Unregulated

By Dave Milliken

£9.99

Unregulated

Other Books in this Series

The Regulators Series

Book 1	**Unregulated**
Book 2	Regulated
Book 3	Pre-Regulated
Book 4	Deregulated

Unregulated

Other Books

My Undocumented Life

The Filing Cabinet

The Digital Wall

Unregulated

Dedication

To my mum.
Love you, mum.

Unregulated

Contents

Contents

Unregulated

Poem: A breed apart

A breed apart,

Where do I start,

I'm a minor in a major key,

Consistent, inconsistently.

Out of sync, covertly misanthropic,

Always current, but always slightly off-topic,

Secure in my doubt, brave in my fear,

Confused or abandoned by all I hold dear.

Listening in vain,

Always chasing comprehension,

But never quite 'in the know',

Like a collapsible wave function.

Unregulated

A stranger in a realm of brothers,

A bastard in a world of mothers,

A null value in an empty set,

The winner in a losing bet.

Empty and full,

Relentless and benign,

In the greater scheme of things,

Is it all just a waste of time?

Eloquent social vampire,

No reflection to behold,

Not comfortable with the masses,

If the truth be bare and told,

Digital obscurity in a digital realm,

Creating my own sanctuary when I don the

helm,

But, alas, when all is said and done,

I can't help but feel that I am always Off by one.

Rejected from The Gentleman Loser,

Understanding what the Chiba City blues are,

Nerves burning out micron by micron,

But unlike Case, I am no cultural icon.

Dave Milliken

9 April 2022

To those who know who they are.

Unregulated

Acknowledgements

I want to offer a massive thank you to all the proof readers who not only took the time to read the first drafts but also offered invaluable corrections.

Annie Shannon

Ashley & Stephen Milliken

Jamie Milliken

Laura Chestnutt

Laurie Cochrane

Unregulated

From the Author

This book is the product of hours and hours of gameplay and reading, and maybe a little bit of experience too.

Games like Dragon Warriors, Dungeons & Dragons, Shadowrun, and Cyberpunk 2077, and reading such books like Shadowrun fiction by a range of authors, Neuromancer by William Gibson, Legend by David Gemmell, and Snow Crash by Neal Stephenson really got me through some tough times moving into and through my teenage years. Later in life, I got a bit of a flavour of the real experience and it was nothing like I expected. Don't get me wrong, I quite enjoyed it, it was just not what my years of game-playing and reading had prepared me for.

So, I guess this book is a homage to what I would have liked that experience to have been like.

On a side note: in true cyberpunk style, I have decided to write this book completely in virtual reality (with the exception of a little bit of editing). Using a Meta Quest 2 headset, the Meta Workrooms app (after about chapter 2, I switched to the much better, Immersed App), and Microsoft Word (I have been trying to prepare myself for the move to Google Docs any day now, but to be fair, I have been preparing myself for such a move for the past 2 years, just haven't "jumped" yet) I have sat in my virtual office and written a novel, my first novel.

Figure 1 My VR work environment

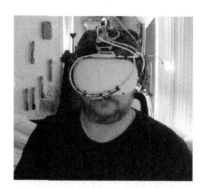

Figure 2 Some idiot wearing a VR headset and trying to write a novel

To be honest, I was blown away by how easy it became to fully engage with my work in this artificial environment. The distractions of the outside world were gone and the desire to check my phone and emails periodically, vanished. I just put on some suitably futuristic music and let my mind and hands do their thing. The weight of the headset disappeared (although I do use the headset a lot, so that may have played a part), for the most part, although I do feel it in my neck the next day.

Don't take it too seriously. It's fun – nothing more.

I hope you enjoy reading it as much as I enjoyed writing it.

Dave Milliken
Belfast
May 2023

From the Author

Unregulated

Introduction

To the average cyberpunk reader, this book really needs no introduction. So, without inadvertently turning this into a "choose your own adventure", if that is you, you can skip this section. See you in Chapter 1.

If you had to Google "cyberpunk" or, heaven forbid, had to refer to an old-fashioned paper-based dictionary then please continue reading. We really need to talk.

I won't get into the whole history of cyberpunk here, but I will say that said history is intriguing and runs further back into the previous century than most people think. But, as far as we are concerned, it takes place in the future. Not usually the distant future with flying cars and holiday trips to outer space, but a closer, more tangible future. A future not completely alien to what we experience today, although usually a little, or a lot, more dystopian.

And while there are any number of cyberpunk books on the market today, this one is a little different.

To my mind, all cyberpunk of this ilk, be it computer games, table top role play games, or fiction, for the most part all, are sourced from the same pool of about 4 or 5 writers.

William Gibson, Bruce Sterling, and Neale Stephenson, while each having their own niche, could be counted amongst these Godfathers of cyberpunk, in my humble opinion, of course. Full in the confidence and understanding that I could never encroach upon the standard that these titans have set and maintain, I did want to add my voice.

So, in the story that follows, you will enter a world set, maybe, fifty years from the time of its writing. A world not so dissimilar to our own, except that people and machines are fused together, not only out of medical necessity, as is currently available right now, but also for the purposes of recreation, functionality, and protection.

I don't focus too heavily on the use of cyberware, as it is affectionately known, certainly not in this novel anyway. But for some of the passages contained within this book to make sense, having an understanding of what cyberware is, even if you don't fully understand the concept, will be a massive help. Most cyberpunk material would be much more explicit.

Another difference that I have included is location. Once again, most alternative material out there will take place on the filthy-chic streets of a glamourous city like Las Vegas or Seattle. I, on the other hand, have selected the aging streets of Belfast, Northern Ireland, a place where I grew up and have lived for a considerable chunk of my adult life.

I haven't gone too crazy with depictions of the political turbulence regarding political borders and the like (I have kept the political situation pretty much as it is currently), but I have included enough local colour to give the reader a bit of an insight into the complications of growing up and living in such an environment.

Submit to your imagination.

Unregulated

Unregulated

Unregulated

Chapter 1: Perfect Planning

Night fell with the ease,
Of a whore to her knees,
While torrential rain,
Tried in vain,
To wash the sins from the city streets.

Dave Milliken

08 May 2019

Hours afterwards, I would tell myself that it all felt wrong from the beginning. If the truth be told, I had always thought this job was the big one, this was the one that was going to get me into the major leagues. But now, there I was, out of ammo and hiding between two dumpsters in a stinking alley, with a price on my head.

They say perfect planning prevents piss poor performance, but I don't know what more I could have done. The rest of my team were either dead, arrested, or heading for the hills, and I probably wouldn't be long behind them. Overhead, a police chopper circled and flashlight beams and the voices of those looking for me were very close by, but they had already checked this alley, so I was safe to ponder my next move. For the moment.

The fabric of the counterfeit police uniform I was wearing was doing nothing to keep the elements at bay. Tonight's wind is starting to cut straight through the flimsy material and I could have sworn I just felt rain.

Next time, if there is a next time, I promised myself that I would spend more money on better quality fake uniforms. I pulled my Beretta pistol clear of its holster and ejected the clip, in case, by some miracle, several rounds of ammunition have appeared there. Sadly not. Feeling naked and ill-prepared, I slapped the clip back in place and return it to my side.

I guess I could have climbed inside a dumpster and waited it out, but I would have rather been off the street, well, I would rather have been in the safe house. But I discarded that idea quickly. I did want to be off the street, but I'm was not going to the safe house. At least one of my team had been arrested and I didn't know how much they have given up - no, the safe house was out of the question. I needed a plan C.

Finally, the night's events seem to be going my way. The chopper did one last sweeping arch above me, before heading off towards the city. It could have just been going to refuel before returning and continuing the search, but I could also hear the raised voices and slamming doors of vehicles as the ground search teams prepared to leave the area. As if to literally piss on my good fortune, it started to rain. Hard.

Two hours later, I was nursing a cup of strong, hot coffee in an all-night diner, contemplating my next move. I swapped my pistol with a homeless man in exchange for the long woollen coat he was wearing. It was surprisingly clean and warm, and absolutely essential to hide my counterfeit attire. I chose this coffee place for its bottomless cups of coffee and the fact that its TV didn't seem to be working, so little chance of my face being recognised from news bulletins - not that I am making the news, mind you. Just trying to cover my ass and not get hypothermia in the process.

The bored waitress approached my table and refilled my coffee cup with all the enthusiasm of someone who was judging her tip by the way I was dressed. I give her the most charming smile I can muster and thanked her, but she ignored me to retake her seat at the counter going back to checking her phone.

I had spent the last hour texting old contacts, anyone with whom I had been out of touch with for at least a year. I didn't know if the cops had my alias yet, but it is less than a year old and unconnected with many previous jobs. This is why they say to never burn an alias if you don't have to, a clean retired one can always be resurrected if needed.

I had my phone answered and to my ear before it could even finish its first ring. I winced, fearing that my enthusiasm might affect my bargaining position. But I am in luck. It's an old contact from Newry, she owes me big time for pulling her out of a firefight between two rival street gangs after they got caught up in a turf war. She was more than happy to cash that favour in now. But, being up to her eyes at the moment, she was also calling in a favour from someone local, a mercenary called Trident. Trident would pick me up, get me off the street and arrange transport wherever I need it, within reason, of course. It is just what I need. I even get some clean hard currency when I push for it. Great! All I had to do now was stay put, and be invisible until Trident arrived in a red Ford Fiesta. I can do that.

Half a cup of coffee later, I see the ancient, gas guzzling Fiesta roll silently to a gentle stop outside the diner. I stood up and swallow down the rest of what can only be described as awful coffee, then, adjusting the long coat for maximum coverage, I slipped a single sheet of the largest unit of currency that I had on me under my cup before making my way to the car. As I got into the Fiesta, I glance back through the diner window at an astonished waitress staring out at me, with an empty coffee cup in one hand and my tip in the other. I smiled. Never judge a book...

I had barely closed the car door when the vehicle starts moving again. Trident was a heavily muscled man, probably in his forties, with a military posture, salt and pepper crew cut, neatly trimmed moustache, and significantly scarred face and hands. He was smartly dressed in a grey shirt, tie, dark grey suit that has been perfectly tailored to help conceal what can only be described as a hand cannon under his left arm, and was wearing a pair of yellowed anti-glare shooting glasses. He never took his eyes off the road while he introduced himself and confirmed for me who had sent him. I started to speak only to be cut off by Trident raising his right hand. We travelled in silence.

The journey was uneventful, although I got spooked when a chopper with its searchlight on, swung overhead. But it was all good. Trident drove carefully and within the law, obviously eager that we didn't attract any unwanted attention from local law enforcement.

We drove for about half an hour before turning into a parking garage and stopping on the third level. I tensed again as I heard a siren wail, but relaxed again as its doppelganger faded to a distant echo.

Trident opened his door and told me to get out. As I stepped out into the cold night air, my charismatic chauffer had pulled a container, of what I guessed to be gasoline, from the trunk.

Had we run out of fuel? Apparently not. He proceeded with covering the vehicle inside and out, with the liquid before putting the container on the passenger seat. I looked on as he lit a cigarette amid a coughing fit - clearly not a smoker - and carefully balanced it on the mouth of the gasoline container.

"Follow me," he said.

I moved quickly to his side, hoping to get away from the stench of fuel and not get caught in the inevitable explosion. Three cars down and the lights of a grey BMW 5 Series flashed twice to indicate the alarm had been disabled.

"Get in" Trident ordered.

Again, I did as I was told, only too aware of the explosion that was imminent. But without any haste, Trident started the car and we rolled out of the high rise. As we accelerated away, a palpable tension left the vehicle when the explosion shook the ground. We both exchanged a relieved glance.

We were gone, virtually untraceable. My night was finally really looking up.

That had all taken place not 18 months ago. It turned out that Trident was looking for work, having just returned from some unwinnable foreign war. He had just been honourably discharged from some abstract branch of the military and was starting to find out the hard way that there were very few legal career paths requiring the ability to kill someone with your bare hands.

But that is where I came in.

I still had a bit of clout and the operational SNAFU that led to our very serendipitous meeting turned out to work in the favour of my client (please don't ask me how) so my reputation was still intact too. It just made sense that we teamed up.

Now, nearly a year and a half later, we were doing good runs, killing bad people (hey, it's all relative), and, most importantly of all, making great money.

Chapter 2: The Killing Room

Tick tock

Tick tock, check the clock,
Sleep is futile, must have shot,
The flock,
Of sheep,
for counting, not for meat,
Too tired to work,
Too awake to sleep.

Dave Milliken

11 September 2017

I stood nervously in the stinking stairwell. Absentmindedly, I let my right hand to drop to pull back the folds of my armoured long coat and briefly caress the pistol grip of my Beretta side arm. It had been stripped, cleaned, oiled, and reassembled in the usual semi-hypnotic haze that I tend to fall into just before a run. In my arms I cradled an ancient and, until recently reliable, Heckler Koch MP-5 submachine gun. This would be its last run. I was fed up faffing around with its loading mechanism and there were much easier options out there. But now I was in position, I gently released the charging handle, supporting it as it chambered the first 9mm round from the magazine, and changed the fire selection switch from "safe" to "burst fire" with two barely audible yet satisfying clicks.

If all was going to plan, Trident, by now, should be dangling precariously outside the only window that serviced this room as a visual connection to the exterior world.

I call it a "run", but I should really call a spade a spade. It was a hit, pure and simple.

Things had become tighter in the running world of late and I had absolutely no idea why. But the usual jobs of extracting Mr(s) Brains from company X and delivering them to organisation Y or stealing covert pieces of military/corporate hardware/software were much fewer and farther between these days. So, here we were.

The plan was simple:

1. Enter the room
2. Kill everyone in the room
3. Leave the room
4. Blow up the room
5. Go home.

What could possibly go wrong with such a well thought out plan?

Not surprisingly, this was Tridents forte, and it was Tridents plan. Quick, clean, and simple was how he liked it.

So, the plan. Well, it was straight out of an old Hollywood movie. A flash bang through the window, closely followed by a hail of bullets courtesy of me and Trident, who would be repelling through said window, just for dramatic effect.

Technically, we were only after one man, Michael Quigley (apparently, he had gotten above his station in some crime syndicate or other) but he was now travelling with 5, er, sorry, I mean 3 security goons (there was an unfortunate misunderstanding at the front door when we were trying to diplomatically negotiate access to the building), so, apparently, they have to go too. When I protest and talk about the sanctity of life, all Trident keeps responding with is that we had a duty to keep it clean (that is Trident code for "no witnesses") and that they knew what they were getting into when they signed up. I am not totally convinced that they did.

The area was a slum, and the building was rundown and in need of more than a bit of work. But it was a mansion compared to the other options in this neighbourhood. The immediate area consisted mostly of small clusters of 4 or 5 rundown terrace bungalows intermittently positioned along one side of the broad litter-strewn street, like reluctant dashes in an emergency morse code message. And on the other, a mixture of semi-detached houses, what use to be green space, and several of these low-profile type apartment buildings.

But the apartment block that served as the Quigley residence stood out from the others. None of the windows were broken and they all had been darkened, the front door was of decent quality and was guarded, and the general space around the building carried an air of "Serious people live here. Squat somewhere else."

In truth, it stuck out like a sore thumb. But here, in this space, confidence was king, and Quigley, if nothing else, was confident.

The radio receiver, that I had recently had surgically implanted in my ear, clicked eerily to life and Tridents calm, deadpan voice echo around the inside of my head clearer than if he had been standing beside me.

"Ok, Blades. I am going to count up to 3 and deploy the stun grenade, just like we planned, just like we have done before. We go on 3, but, do not move, I repeat, do not move until after you hear the bang. Understand?"

I rolled my eyes. Anybody else might have been quite insulted at such a stupid utterance except, a couple of months ago, there had been an "incident". In my defence, I have jacked up reflexes and he didn't specify that I shouldn't go on 3 but on the beat after 3 (which is technically

4). But I reluctantly answered in the affirmative through my throat mic.

Trident started to count, "1…2…"

I heard the window smash followed by the shouts and grunts of a surprised security team, then BANG! The gap between the door and the floor lit the entire stairwell up like a firework in a cave. I made my move.

The door was unlocked and swung open under the force of my boot. Everyone in the room had turned their focus, understandably, towards the window, or at least, where the window once had been. Four people stood, like frozen statues, blinded by the phosphorous chemical reaction, and now, finally, began fumbling for their weapons.

It wasn't just from neat rows of cans and bottles, of indeterminate remaining volume or the strong smell of cannabis in the air, that suggested some quantity of drink and drugs had been enjoyed here this evening, but the slow reactions of what I can only assume were highly trained professionals crumbled under the weight of the assault.

I raised the MP-5 and let it sing in the key of 3 round bursts. The new sound of singing death, trailing their collective attention away from the window and towards where I stood near, but not in, the door way. The bullets were the notes, and screams and shouting were the vocals as the dance began in earnest. But not a sound from me, I was the conductor.

Bullets ripped through the air, tearing at clothing and skin and paint-peeling plaster walls, the closeness of proximity rendering their shoddy, low grade body armour virtually useless.

But it was too late. They were either too drunk, or too high, or too slow, or too surprised, or some combination of all 4, because they fell were they stood.

It wasn't until the shooting stopped and the smoke cleared that we could finally survey the damage and identify Quigley.

He was dead. So were his security team. Nice and clean. Just like we'd planned. Just the way Trident liked it.

I took a hi-res photo of Quigley and sent it through a pre-agreed encrypted messaging app to our client and got, what I considered to be totally inappropriate, 2 thumbs up emojis in reply.

Mission accomplished.

We dragged the almost-lifeless, moaning and gurgling, bodies of the 2 guards we had dealt with at the front door, to join Quigley and their comrades (no one should have to die alone), then we left the building. Trident only pausing long enough to place a small incendiary charge to destroy what was left of the room and its occupants.

We crossed the street and I systematically started to disarm our weapons and place them into a large, black, canvass gym bag, before placing the bag carefully inside the trunk. Trident passed me his pump action shotgun, which was already empty (Trident was a proud and vocal non-subscriber to the single-bullet theory), while he gathered up his climbing ropes and wound them into a neat bundle. It all went into the gym bag too.

I smiled despite myself as I took a glance up and down the virtually empty street. 1 flash bang had been deployed, 24 rounds of 9mm and at least five 12-gauge cartridges had been discharged, and 6 people had died. But not one resident batted an eyelid. Not one.

The sound of gunfire and screaming were never far away in a neighbourhood like this and, these days, there seemed to be more and more neighbourhoods like this. The cops didn't care for the people who lived here and would rarely even respond if you did take the time, and your life in your hands, to call them.

As if on cue, a rattle of gun fire and shouting erupted from one of the streets close by. Not close enough to make me react, but close enough to drag my attention back from my musings and to the job at hand. Trident had already gotten into the passenger seat and put his seatbelt on (safety first) when I climbed behind the steering wheel and started the ignition. Before moving off, I passed my phone to Trident. It was a burner and the only number the client could contact us on. The explosive charge Trident had planted before leaving the killing room detonated before we even had left the street.

And, as we entered the light evening traffic, some semblance of normality descended upon us, the burner phone bleeped twice. With a huge smile on his face, my partner in literal crime, informed me that we had just been paid.

Chapter 3: A Clean Getaway

Night fell quickly,
and the Morning laughed.

Dave Milliken

15 February 2019

It was one of those nights. You know the ones. The day had been stinking hot, like so hot you could theoretically fry an egg on the pavement. But as darkness fell, a cool breeze cleared the suffocating, muggy air and replaced it with something fresh and revitalising. All the thoughts of the evening's events and the grisly scene back at Quigleys had been temporarily forgotten. Our spirits were high and our bank accounts were full, well, fuller than they had been.

We drove on. With the windows down, music slightly louder than was usual (we didn't play our music loud, Trident insisted, as it dulled our combat intuition), and a cool breeze in our hair.

As we approached our safehouse, Trident lowered the music to a more "combat sense"-friendly level. I felt the, almost imperceivable, tension start to rise in my friend as we both fell into a hyper awareness of our surroundings.

When you have a target on your back, it is commonly considered that you are most vulnerable when entering or leaving cover/concealment[1], a fact we both knew only too well. That cover/concealment could be anything from a building, a dark shadowed area, or a vehicle.

---

[1] Cover will protect you from small arms fire even if the enemy can see you.
Concealment will protect you from being seen by the enemy but not provide protection against small arms fire.

As usual, we over shot our destination by about 2 blocks and then doubled back, constantly on the lookout for anything that might seem out of place.

We had a golden rule: if it feels wrong, it is wrong.

But on this occasion, it all felt good, or at least it felt normal. So, I parked the rental car a street away and collected the gym back from the trunk. And then, together, we made our way to the apartment we had rented in cash, on a daily basis, for the past week.

The front door to the building itself was broken, but it had been broken since the day we started our rental agreement, and the lobby stank of urine, and was littered with garbage, which sat at odds with the stained, peeling, lemon yellow paint job. There was a relatively small reception area, complete with a concrete desk and even a small backroom office, as if, in its hay day, this building had sported a security guard or receptionist or, at least, aspired to.

Our landlady, Rita, was the nervous sort, but had the stones to show up and rent in person, a rare thing these days. As far as she was concerned, we were travelling artists who just needed somewhere to crash while our exhibition was on display at a local art house.

Up until our occupancy, the backroom had been used by the homeless on occasion, and we were both torn on the topic of ejecting them back onto the street. Anyone can fall on hard times and sometimes all someone needed was a place to sleep, some clean clothes, and access to decent personal hygiene facilities to get them back on track. But, unfortunately, the homeless tended to bring crime and crime brought attention. We needed neither. So, on our first night, we made an example of our unofficial lodger, Memo, and sent him on his way. Don't misunderstand me, we didn't kill him, just, well, we re-educated him and that sort of news travels fast. There were easier places to sleep than this.

I paid a working girl to collect Memo from the emergency care facility where he went to seek treatment for his injuries, and then take him to a flophouse where I had prepaid his stay for a month, and the working girl could give him the night of his life!

Trident had rolled his eyes once he had worked out what I had done, informing me, for the millionth time, that I couldn't save everyone. This always made me smile. He was such a pessimist.

Upon our arrival, and as per the rental agreement, we had changed the front door and locks to something that wouldn't fall down during a stiff breeze. To be honest, the landlady, Rita, almost seemed to be relieved when she first met us to look the place over. It was cheap and convenient, but most importantly, she would never breathe a word that we had stayed there, no matter who was asking.

Once we had disarmed the locks (which were definitely showing signs that they were tampered with during our short absence), and disarmed the small, but deadly, explosive proximity charge (in case the locks didn't do their job), we headed inside to start the cleanup in earnest.

It was a single room split into two by (surprisingly clean) carpet and lino to act as a living space/bedroom and small kitchen area. In the back left corner was a boarded off area which serviced as both shower and toilet. The entire apartment had been freshly painted grey and contained no furniture or utilities (except the shower and toilet, of course).

Like a surgeon before a complicated operation, I pulled on a pair of non-latex gloves, then stripped of my armoured long coat, being careful not to let it touch the ground and hung It on a coat hanger on the back of our new front door. From a sealed bag I had in my pocket, I removed a thick yellow plastic bag adorned with the red 6 horned symbol that warned of biohazardous materials.

Piece by piece, I carefully removed each item of my clothing and placed it into the bag. Everything I had been wearing that evening went into the bag. Looking over to where Trident had been doing the same thing, I could only see his pile of clothing. Having more practice with these sorts of precautions, he was already in the shower, singing in a key that would be a mystery to even the most tone-deaf of karaoke performers. He had placed his clothing neatly and carefully upon another plastic bag, obviously to prevent contact with the floor. I stowed these clothes into the bag they were sitting on and then placed it into the biohazard bag.

Finally, expertly peeling off the surgical gloves and carefully placing them into the bag as well, I pulled the self-sealing cord at the neck of the bag. There was a satisfying sizzle as the yellow biohazard bag became hermetically sealed.

Just as I was finishing up, Trident emerged from the shower space with a fluffy white towel around his waist. His well-defined muscles rippled as he walked. And as he walked there was no wasted movement. It was almost a dance.

"Shower is all yours", he smiled, then added, "I've used all the hot water."

I smiled inwardly. This was his idea of a joke, but I tutted dutifully, like a spoiled teenager, in response and he laughed out loud. But there was truth to this joke; he will have used all the hot water.

I emerged from my refreshing but very cold shower, having washed every surface and crevasse of myself thoroughly with a soap that really blared the line between detergent and caustic soda.

Trident had already taken the time to clean and decontaminate our armoured long coats. He was now dressed in a kaki sports jacket, blue jeans, and black polo neck, and was now stripping and cleaning the weapons used in tonight's expedition.

The one thing they forget to tell you when you enter the gun for hire business is that blood, brains, skin, and miscellaneous tissue gets everywhere. And I mean everywhere. Taking the time, if possible, to get clean after an operation was essential if you wanted to preserve your freedom and ultimately, your life. If you fail to do so, sooner or later, it will all catch up with you and an incompetent justice system will use your conviction and incarceration as proof of their dedication and competence. Or you might even draw the ire of a local criminal enterprise or two.

Once out of the shower, I dressed. Black dress fatigues, a dark grey armoured t-shirt, and grey military style boots. The new radio mic implanted in my ear was still an irritation, but its function and effectiveness overruled this concern. I took some time to critic myself in front the full-length steel mirror that had been bolted to the wall. I stood at 6 foot 3 inches tall and had a rangy frame that bordered on skinny. Short, black, messy hair, a triangular jaw line, and augmented grey eyes reflected back at me. With a flex of my forearms, 3, four-inch razor sharp claws extended from their ports on the back my of hands. These were new, and up until this point, unused. But I loved the feeling when they slid out and locked in place.

Without a word, I put on my long coat, grabbed the biohazard bag, and left the apartment. As I did so, I heard Trident ring the car rental company and report our vehicle as stolen.

But this was the routine. This is how we operated. This is how we stayed one or two steps ahead of the law, and, more importantly, ahead of the competing and warring companies and crime syndicates (although it was often difficult to tell these 2 factions apart).

A twenty-minute drive later and I had incinerated the biohazard bag with the assistance from an old friend who I used to work the graveyard shift in a recycling plant. Then, on a generic street, in a generic part of the city, I pulled over, put the vehicle in park, and turned off the engine. I did my best to cover the fact that I was coating the inside of the vehicle with petrol, but nobody cared anyway. In a crude and ham-fisted fashion, I did my best to imitate the local beginner car booster. I ripped away the ignition column and start to play with the wiring. By some happy accident, something went wrong, and a spark from the wiring started a small fire on the gasoline-soaked passenger seat. I quickly stepped away, slamming the driver door closed. This is not my car and not my business. The fire grew and grew as I watched from the opposite side of the street until the vehicle was totally engulfed in flames. But no one cared. It was just another burnt out car in another burnt out neighbourhood.

A block away, I disarmed the alarms on my pride and joy, a Honda XL750 motorbike. Retrieving the helmet from the storage box, I put it on, started the bikes engine, and made my way back to the safe house.

It was time to get some rest.

Chapter 4: A New Day

Alcohol-soaked tourists,
With full wallets but empty minds,
Frequent soulless venues,
Seeking fulfilment in the mundane.

Dave Milliken

17 May 2019

My eyes flicked open.

The room was very dark, but my implanted low-light compensators made up the difference. I reached over and checked the time on my phone. 0447hrs. Rolling off the inflatable mattress that had served me as a bed for the past week or so, I dressed quickly in the dark. I could hear the subdued snoring of Trident, letting me know that he was still asleep. He would be really annoyed if I woke him. So, as soon as I had brushed my teeth, splashed some water around my face, and put my sidearm in a shoulder rig, I grabbed my long coat and quietly headed out the door.

The streets were virtually empty as I emerged from the apartment building. The morning air was cool and peaceful and, being summer, the sun was threatening to break over the horizon any moment now. But it was still bright and clear. The main sound breaking the silence was the call of the seagulls as they soared between the high-rise buildings looking to make a meal of some discarded fast-food container or another. This would soon be replaced by the essential workforce of the city, the cleaners, bakers, truck drivers, retail and hospitality staff, and the over-enthusiastic office workers, making their way to their place of employment, or their next delivery. A noisy, beeping, street sweeping vehicle irreverently broke the morning chorus and could now be heard the next street over, meticulously carving its way up one side of the pavement and down the other. And tomorrow, at the same time and in the same place, it could be found doing the exact same thing. To think that people used to actually drive those things, it was mind boggling!

This is what it felt like, to me at least, when a city woke up.

I headed, on foot, to an all-night diner, just on the edge of the city centre, where I knew I could get a decent coffee and a good breakfast. I had become a sort of regular in the short space of time that we had rented the safe house in the area, and it always felt good to be greeted by the familiar wait staff. But it was more than that. Places like this were an oasis for people like me. I knew, that, if in a week's time, someone, official or unofficial, where to come around asking questions about me, my movements, or my habits, the entire compliment of staff, including their surveillance equipment, would develop a severe and persistent case of amnesia.

They just never knew who frequented places like this, especially at weird times of the day and night, so it was always the better policy not to take the risk with sharing information on patrons. And, with the exception of law enforcement, most criminal organisations and corporations, over the years, seemed to respect this.

In the end, what you were left with was almost hallowed ground. In the history of this city, back when the violence and mayhem was much easier to understand, it was understood that if you were given asylum by the church of your particular side, you could ask the priest, the minister, or the pastor to intercede on your behalf. But, while you were on hallowed ground you were safe from physical harm – from your own side, at least. So, it reminded me of those days, only with many more exceptions and many more shades of grey.

As I entered "The Breakfast Shack" I was greeted by a young male server, Ben, who knew me as Jack.

"Good morning, Jack.", he said, cheerily, "And how is the world of international finance?"

It was a fair, if not weird question. As far as Ben was concerned, I was an international banker working in commodities in the central business district, hence the weird visiting hours, and I was here, technically, on my lunch break.

"Good morning, Ben", I smiled back as I took a seat in the far corner of the diner, beside a window, but with my back to the wall, "Exploiting the poor and the oppressing the masses as per usual"

He laughed that forced laugh that people, who are depending on your tip, tend to laugh. "Do you need a menu? Or are you going to order your usual?"

"I will have the usual, one Ulster fry, if you don't mind, Ben. And keep the coffees coming."

Ben did a fake salute and busied himself with the order.

It was a large, L-shaped diner, with multiple points of cover and concealment, and a clear exit through the front or through the back, using the kitchen. I sat in a booth at the back wall, close to the window and next to the door that led to that kitchen. This morning it was only sparsely populated, and with no one that I particularly remember from previous visits.

My coffee arrived with the efficiency I tended to expect from this place, so I settled down, with my phone before me, and started to look for new jobs.

Given the nature of my work it was important to remain as anonymous as you could, right up until payday, if possible. This meant that I had to use the commonly misunderstood dark web.

So, this takes me onto a tangent...

It had been explained to me by woman called Angie. Angie had issues with people, big issues. But one of the most prominent issues was the internet. Or at least, peoples understanding of the internet. The fact that, in this day and age, people still don't understand the difference between the web and the internet astounded her. It astounded her that people aren't even just a little bit curious about something that they literally rely on in their work and home life, yet have such a vague understanding what it is.

So, let me explain it to you like Angie explained it to me.

The internet and the **World Wide Web** (hence the initialism **WWW**, also just known as "**the web**") are not the same thing. Much in the same way that cars and roads are related, but the words cannot be used interchangeably.

The internet (the physical architecture) is like the railway tracks, and the World Wide Web (the bit you access through your browser) is like a train. The train can run on the tracks, but it is not the only train that can. The web is a service. Other services, like file transfer (FTP, or file transfer protocol), and email (e.g. SMTP, or Simple Mail Transfer Protocol), can also be run on these tracks.

And just a quick word on the dark web. There are 3 main, and industry recognised, levels to the web.

You have the **surface web**. This is the bit you can "see". If you open your favourite browser, use your favourite search engine, and type in a search string and click search. That! That is the surface web. The results you receive will be from the surface web. Without getting too technical, a website needs to be "discovered" and its contents "understood" by a search engine before it can be displayed in a search result. As a result of this, the majority of the web is known as the deep web.

The **deep web** consists of every website that has been created but not indexed by a search engine. This might be intentional as it might contain or act as a portal to sensitive or private information.

The **dark web** is another matter, but don't believe all the hype. While it still runs on the internet, it requires a special (and free) browser to do so. You cannot find yourself on the dark web by accident. And while you can buy drugs, guns, and other illicit items and services, for the most part, it is just the same as the surface and deep web, but without the incessant tracking and advertising (and a little bit more anonymity).

So, back to business...

I flicked through a couple of message boards, highlighting, saving, and sending expressions of interest for jobs that might have been suitable, but if the truth be told, nothing really jumped out at me.

I finished my breakfast and spent some time touching base with friends and associates. Sending a meme here and a "How are you keeping?" there. It may not sound like much, but it kept your name on their mind. And while we were fresh from a recent payday, that money would not last as long as we would like, so I was looking for the next gig.

Ben had now been joined by the day shift staff, two attractive looking women, who were busy getting up to speed on what their duties might be for today. I wasn't as familiar with them, but they seemed to be grand enough.

Ben came to bus my table, and, after thanking him for the breakfast, I, as I had numerous times before, asked for a take away container of porridge, made with water, not milk. From behind his back, he produced a container of porridge. I smiled, thanked him, and after taking care of the bill and leaving a generous tip, headed back to the safe house.

I checked the time as I headed back. 0630hrs. Trident would be up and about and looking forward to his porridge.

I entered the apartment to find Trident, as expected, up and dressed. He was lying on his mattress and reading from his phone as I came into the main room.

He looked up as I entered and asked "You didn't bring home any porridge, did you?" His face brightened when I tossed him the container which he caught smartly.

He opened the lid and, with a satisfied look on his face and breathed in the smell of contents deeply. His bliss was temporarily interrupted when a frown crossed his brow, "Is made with…"

We finished the sentence in chorus "…water, not milk? Yes, it is made with water, not milk." I said rolling my eyes at his fastidiousness.

"You are the best, Blades", he managed, as he started to devour the containers contents.

I took a seat on the end of my makeshift bed and pulled the canvass bag, containing our weapons from last night, closer. Unzipping the bag, I could smell the aroma of gun oil, hard graft, and death.

I pulled clear my empty MP-5 submachine gun free and carried out a visual and physical inspection to ensure that the weapon was unloaded and empty. Then, using a manoeuvre, famous the world over, I slapped the charging handle down allowing it to slide forward. There was no magazine in the weapon, so nothing was loaded into the breach, but I still found the action very satisfying, although it was feeling much more loose, and more than a little bit gritty. Pulling the charging handle back again, I locked it in position and it immediately slid forward, unable to grip on the worn-down metal crevice that should hold it in place. I pursed my lips. This was not optimal. Unfortunately, even after servicing the weapon many times, the locking mechanism was becoming a bit hit and miss. And recently it was more miss than hit.

"You still thinking about changing it?" Trident asked, between licks of the excess porridge on the container lid.

"Yeah," I replied, feeling more than a bit torn. "Just can't trust that locking mechanism anymore."

Trident nodded, "We best go and see your 'friend', Laura." He even did the air quotes and everything.

Chapter 5: Tools of the Trade

Under foreign skies,
A raised head,
Meets almond eyes,
A soul so beautiful,
And deep,
A lightning strike,
A quantum leap.

Dave Milliken
17 May 2019

The conversation had been very brief, mostly one sided, and entirely through an encrypted texting app. But Laura had agreed to see me and we even managed to set a time for the afternoon later that same day. She even allowed Trident to tag along too, weapons dealers are notoriously paranoid.

So, at 1430hrs, we walked through the busy Belfast streets towards the central business district in silence.

In the middle of the tall, shiny buildings, under the nose of the oblivious strait-laced corporate wage slaves that travelled these streets every weekday, in a broad uninviting alley, tucked away and concealed behind a dilapidated wooden fence, stood a night club that only those 'in the know' actually knew about. There was no signage or advertising, no brights light or pizzazz, just the promise of exclusivity and relative anonymity. And admission was granted by invitation only.

Thompsons Garage, affectionately known as just "Thompsons" had been a fixture in the lore of Belfast's seedy underbelly for, at least, the past 50 years, perhaps even a bit longer. Thumbing its nose at the new world order that had engulfed its surroundings, it stood, defiantly, as a sort of relic to a more humble past. An open secret, of sorts, amongst the locals and its frequenters.

But as well as serving the community as an illegal nightclub located in the very centre of the most respectable area of the city, it also operated as a front of possibly one of the most prolific arms dealers in Europe. It was always worth remembering that.

The huge steel, rusting, front sliding door was almost as famous as the location itself, to those who knew, of course. It was ajar as we approached.

Laura had some rules to attending her place of business. Firstly, don't show up unannounced. While she could distinguish the difference between someone lost and looking to use the bathroom and someone with more 'professional' intentions, it wasn't going to end well for either, it would just be a question of severity. Two, no weapons in her temple of weapons. No guns, no knives, no batons, whips, chains… well, you get the idea. The sharpest thing you could carry, that would be acceptable, would be your wit, and you should definitely bring your sharpest wit. And three, no uninvited guests. Don't bring anyone with you that hadn't been OK'ed by Laura in advance. Either one of you, or both of you would not be having a good day after that. These rules were enforced to the letter and, if rumours served correctly, there are no shortage of stories emphatically illustrating why they should not be broken.

I gave Trident one last reassuring nod and took the lead. Even just stepping through the sliding door was an assault on the senses. Moving from the bright sunny daylight outside into the dark and murky bowels, of what was essentially a warehouse kitted out with a bar and some gangways, was a struggle even for my light compensators. And then there was the smell. The stench of stale beer, sweat, cigarette smoke, blood, excitement, and bleach hung heavily in the air. And the noise, or lack of it. It seemed just wrong to enter a place like this and there to be no noise. It almost felt like you were being suffocated by silence. But you can't operate an illegal nightclub, in the middle of the central business district of a vibrant and active city, for half a century, if you don't understand the basics of acoustics and soundproofing.

At first glance, the place looked empty. But I put my hands up regardless and announced myself in a loud, clear voice.

"Afternoon, Laura. Full disclosure, ", I continued, slowly walking forward and scanning the terrain in front of me, she would know we were here, and was probably watching us via some hidden camera as I spoke, "I've had some hand razors fitted since the last time we met and I am not sure how I can leave them at home."

"That is so cliché, Blades!". The gentle, feminine voice came from just behind us and I turned to see Laura, all of 5 foot 2 inches of her, and heavily pregnant, standing with her trademark half-smile on her manga-esque face. She carried a scar on her left cheek, from breaking up a knife fight in her younger days of running an unlawful discothèque, but she declared that it was a badge of honour and point blank refused to get the 15-minute cosmetic surgery to remove it. She was a well-proportioned woman for her size and wore her fringed, long black hair up in a pony tail most days. Forever a tomboy at heart, she wore grey fatigues, grey military-style boots, and an off-white form fitting t-shirt that rode up over her swollen belly. Oh...and she was flanked by 2 security goons.

"Oh my God! What happened to you?", I exclaimed staring at her extended belly, genuine shock on my face and amazement in my voice.

Her smile broadened, "I am growing up and settling down, Blades. That is what people our age usually to do!" Breaking her own protocol, she charged forward and embraced me tightly. Well, half embraced me, half patted me down for additional weapons. She released me and backed up a little, then taking both my hands in hers and looking me straight in the eye, "How are you keeping? It has been too long."

I tried to keep smiling and maintain my calm as I realised, she was running her thumbs over the ports of my hand razors. One accidental flex from me, and this meeting would be over before it started. "I am good. I am good.", I stammered, "You know the deal. I have a constant need to hustle.", I shrugged, "This is my partner, Trident.", I gestured to Trident with my chin, whose full attention was taken up with Laura's entourage. It was tense moment, but Trident finally submitted to a pat down by one of the security guys.

Laura's smile faded a little as she looked at Trident, but didn't move. "Nice to meet you,

Trident. OK, boys. You have looked scary for long enough. Go back to your duties."

Both men nodded to me, gave Trident the stink eye and then disappeared through some random door.

"Shall we?", Laura led me by the hand deeper into the nightclub. I allowed myself to be guided as Trident followed along behind, diligently watching our 6. I am not a mind reader, nor am I a betting man, but by the look on his face, I am pretty sure he was regretting not bringing his gun.

We continued to catch up, the conversation being light and jovial as we descended a long course of metal warehouse stairs, lit with blue neon tubes set into the crevasse between the wall and the ceiling, into a basement. It was much better lit down here and resembled some form of workshop.

It was a large, open space, maybe 60 metres by 20 metres, with long steel, standing-height work benches set up in rows, filling the room and lining the perimeter walls. It all looked very clean and perhaps even a bit clinical. The lighting hung from the ceiling in florescent tubes, giving a semblance of daylight.

"So, who knocked you up?", I asked, a bit out of the blue and a bit too serious.

Laura smiled again, the trademark smile, "As tactful as ever, Johnathan?". I winced, no one ever used my real name, in fact, very few people even knew it. But she only giggled at my discomfort and lowered her head and looked at me through her fringe then said, in a sultry voice, "You had the opportunity to make an honest woman of me, didn't you?". I winced again.

"You know it just wasn't meant to be *that way* between us, don't you.", I answered sheepishly.

She laughed and brightened. "I know. You made the hard choice for us both. I can see that now.", she stepped forward and kissed me lightly on the cheek, her trademark smile turning into something genuine and warm." Anyway, ", she continued, lightening the mood, "Went to the clinic.", then in a false deep voice she declared, "I don't need no man!" and she laughed. I laughed too, but it was more of a nervous laughter. She was still as wild as ever.

Trident looked as uncomfortable as I felt.

"So, things have changed around here, too. By the looks of things", I said, gazing around the room and desperate to change the subject of conversation.

Just then, what I assume was an employee, in casual civilian clothing descended the stairs and politely knocked the wall, in absence of a door, and looked inquisitively at Laura. "Would you guys like a drink?" Laura asked.

I nodded, "Sure, I would love a latte, and Trident will have a tea, the weirder the better, if you got one." The personal assistant or barback or whatever they were, smiled, nodded, and disappeared as quickly as they had arrived.

"Doesn't he speak for himself?", Laura asked, nodding in Tridents direction and furrowing her brow.

"He's shy." I joked. "So, what is this place?" Again, trying to get the conversation back to the reason we were actually here.

"We are diversifying. Someone once told me, if you aren't moving forward, you are moving backward.", that someone was me, "So, we use to use this place for, well, you know.", I did not know, but I let her continue without interruption, "But it is becoming harder and harder to co-exist in that market with the local venders without forcing someone's hand and starting a turf war. A war that we would undoubtedly win, but not before spilling a lot of loyal blood on both sides and developing a lot of ill will towards our general enterprise.", she paused as our drinks arrived, were distributed, and the courier had disappeared again, "We have been in talks with local people and local authorities and are looking for a more legal means to serve the community."

To be honest, I had very little clue as to what she was talking about, but I would assume it was drugs. I heard that her organisation had stopped dealing altogether. The local paramilitaries had their steel fist around the dealing scene, so I can only suppose that is what she was talking about. "So, you are getting out of the arms business, too?", I enquired over the rim of my takeaway coffee cup.

Another smile kissed Laura's lips and she laughed gently, "Oh no. The weapons business is too good. And the nightclub, well we keep that more for our connection with the local community, or should I say, communities. This will be something different. Something grander. Something that adds value.", she emphasised the point by making a little circle motion with her cup, then taking a sip. "But that is not why you are here, is it?"

"It all sounds very exciting, and more than a bit confusing. But no, that is not why I am here."

"Well," she replied, "step into my office", and with that she motioned that we should follow her to a steel, reinforced door that was hidden in a recess of the wall. She sent a message from her phone, and within seconds a series of locks and bolts were disengaged and the door before us swung open.

I just want to make it clear that transactions with Laura were not always this weird and/or complicated. In fact, it would usually be very straight forward. I would contact Laura and agree a place to meet. At the meet, I would tell her what I needed, she would tell me what she had available and we would haggle on price. I would then pay 10% upfront to show my commitment to the deal. A week or so later, she would let me know where to meet, I would transfer the remainder of the balance and she would give me my new toy. Job done!

But as I stepped into the new room, I was hit by a wall of cool, dry, air and I could see that Laura's fortunes were indeed on the verge of changing, if they had not changed already.

The room was dimly lit with up shielded fluoresces mounted on the wall, and the hum of a climate control system buzzed in the background. While it was a much smaller room, about 20 metres by 20 metres, it was racked with guns, of virtually every variety, and gun accessories, on every wall and a maze of weapons racks in the middle of the room. She was showing off, trying to impress me, but wow, had she impressed me. Two employees, I assume, in white lab coats and carrying clipboards who had, once again, I assume, opened the door from the inside, completely ignored us and went back to taking inventory or whatever it was they were doing.

"Did you have anything in mind?" She said, knowing the spectacle will have overwhelmed me. "Nothing is loaded, so feel free to touch and sample the wares. Usual mate's rates apply. All sales are final. I would also appreciate it if you could wear gloves before touching anything. We have a courtesy box in the corner. It is for your safety and for ours."

Trident fished two sealed bags each containing a pair of non-latex surgical gloves from his inside pocket. He tossed a pair to me, and, as instructed by our host, we put them on.

Trident cautiously entered into the room gazing around in wonder. He placed his empty tea cup on an empty workspace desk and then, growing in confidence, started to pace the racks, occasionally stopping to test the charging action and sight alignment of this weapon or that. It was truly like watching a kid in a toy store, being allowed to pick one thing, only one thing, but it could be anything they liked. The idea or seeing and touching a weapon before you bought it was virtually unheard of in our line of work. When you received you purchase it was up to you to assess its viability. On more than one occasion, I have purchased items that turned out to be less than useless. And that was when I met and started to buy from Laura.

I am not a drinker, but I found myself in Thompsons one evening after a successful run. I had no idea who she was. She was part of a small team I was working with that evening and was she introduced to me as 'Jill'. I later discover the fact that she was, what we would call in the game, a fixer, AKA a solver of supply problems and on that particular evening, my employer.

She provided quality weapons, ammunition, and equipment, and she refused to compromise on that. It was I who pursued the relationship further, and I who fundamentally broke it off. But Laura was a professional, and would never let emotion or personal affairs interfere with what was most important to her: making money and building an empire.

I walked along one wall of rifles running my gloved finger along the steel bracing. I needed something to replace my MP-5. So, I was looking something short for clearing rooms, but also something more tactical[2] and that packed a more powerful punch if possible. This usually came in the form of a picatinny rail that was a standard rail onto which attachments could be fastened. The more powerful punch would usually result in opting for a larger calibre, but that can lead to ammunition supply problems.

I stopped. Part of me thought I would be purchasing a MP-5 today, the tactical version, but still an MP-5. But, like I had said before, the reloading mechanism was really starting to grind my gears. So, when I saw her, you can imagine my excitement and surprise. I pulled the rifle clear of the rack to feel its weight in my hands, then I pulled it to my shoulder, working the charging mechanism, looking down the sights, feeling for the mode selector switch, safety (which was built into the trigger), and manoeuvrability.

---

[2] The word "tactical" is just military code for "supports more toys" like a laser sight or a torch.

Laura appeared at my shoulder, "Ah, the ADS Amphibious assault rifle? Nice choice. Developed by Russia in the 2010's for use by their special forces. Using special rounds, this unit can actually be fired under water. This particular model has been chambered for 762 NATO rounds and is effective up to around 500 metres. Compared to the 9mm rounds, this will make the MP-5 feel like an air rifle. We have re-tuned it to make it more effective and accurate out of the water, but this, in turn effects its underwater accuracy. The bullpup loading mechanism makes the rifle shorter and more portable, without compromising on power. This rifle will come with 3x 45-round capacity magazines, empty of course, but additional 30 round mags and 50 or 100 round drum mags are available upon request. If you want the magazines preloaded, let us know and we can handle that. It has a picatinny rail mounted on the carrying handle for attaching sights, a laser, and/or a torch. It is threaded for a suppressor or compensator and also comes with a built in 40mm caseless grenade launcher. With the exception of the grenade launcher, these will, of course, come at an additional cost, but I am sure we can work something out a price where we are all happy. Both types of ammunition I can source and supply, in reasonable quantities, within 24 hours, that is if I don't already have them in stock, which we probably will." Tridents eye brows raised so high they almost left his forehead.

"I'll take it. It will be like an early Christmas present from me to me.", I said.

"Would you like it gift wrapped?" Laura teased.

Chapter 6: The Favour

A bar, lightly scattered,
With the persistent,
Or the lost,
A raised voice,
Barbed with angry words,
Breaks a silence that never was.

Dave Milliken
17 May 2019

Trident selected some accessories, a three-point sling, a new sound suppressor for his SMG, and a previously loved scope. And after a lot of haggling, I think everyone felt like they had gotten the best deal they could. And so, we headed back up the stairs and on to the nightclub floor.

But there was something on Laura's mind. The passing stranger or acquaintance probably would not have noticed, but I had known her for years and it was very apparent. At first, I thought it might have been the excitement of showing off her new business expansion. But the negotiations were now done, prices had been agreed, and money and merchandise had exchanged hands. Or, at least, would be delivered within the next 24 hours.

"What's on your mind, Laura?" I asked, in a low voice, but loud enough so that she would hear me.

She opened her mouth to protest innocence, then closed it again, looked me in the eye, and sighed, "I never could hide anything from you, could I? Could I take another couple of minutes of your precious time?"

I shrugged and smiled then looked over at Trident. He also shrugged and nodded. "Sure, what's up?" I responded, furrowing my brow in concern. This was not normal protocol for Laura.

5 minutes later, we find ourselves in yet another obscure part of Thompsons Garage. This time we are upstairs, and the room is very lavish. Decorated wooden panels line the walls, lit with fixtures and fitting that would be very at home in the previous century. A massive wooden desk sits at one end of a large, bright, carpeted room, maybe about 10 metres squared, with a plush executive office chair behind it. The desk is furnished with an ancient handheld phone, the type that had physical buttons and needed to be plugged into a wall, and various reports and memos were placed neatly in, what I can only assume was, "to be done" and "done" piles.

Laura, now flanked by a personal assistant named "Steve", was sitting behind the desk, no longer with the air of the fragile young pregnant woman I had loved with reckless abandon many years ago. This was Laura the business woman, the weak persona no longer needed to extract the best price from a duped customer.

Steve, the personal assistant, was a large guy, the type of guy that never missed a meal and probably wasn't keen on sharing food either. He stood about 6 foot 3 inches tall and had a belly that only an over indulgence in beer could provide. But he carried himself well, stood with good posture, and definitely gave off the air "I am a lover not a fighter, but when it comes down to it, I love to fight". He wore a smart, well-tailored, dark blue suit, a white shirt, and matching bowtie. He was calm and courteous in a way that only those with the skills and experience and zero fear can be. And, while I couldn't see it from here, I would guess that he was definitely armed.

"My family had owned this site for the past 100 years." Her voice was still soft, but any hint of fragility had disappeared, her eyes were down towards the desk, and she absentmindedly tapped a pen against some paperwork as if to emphasis what she was saying. "And in that time, we have served all the local communities, regardless of religion or political persuasion, in their need for illicit chemicals, alcohol, and a place to consume them comfortably that existed outside the violent political backdrop and calls for civil war.

"When my dad died, and I took over, I made sure that we maintained our neutral and detached political position. We were an oasis for all. A place to come when your world got too real, a place to unwind from the aloof day to day crime of common or garden terrorism, a place to commit the only crime", she made air quotes, "worth committing, the crime of self-gratification".

Thompsons Garage would be born out of the days of a Christian fundamentalist approach to governance. Did you know that?"

I shrugged, I did not know that, and neither, apparently, did Trident.

She continued "The Northern Irish state drinking laws were draconian and enforced with an iron fist. We, "she waved the pen in a rough circle in front of her," were on the frontline challenging that." I shot a bemused glance at Trident and Laura smiled to herself, realising that she was going off a rant rather than dealing with the issue at hand. "But I digress...

"I have an issue. An issue with a local paramilitary commander who has his sights set on turning this place, my home, into some form of paramilitary gathering place.

"I won't have it. I won't have the impartiality that we have worked so hard for all these years, destroyed, all because of the ambition of one overambitious fool."

"So, you would like him 'removed'?", Trident spoke for the first time. Finally, we were on a topic that interested him. I tried to surreptitiously catch his eye to show my displeasure. But I got the distinct impression that he was deliberately ignoring me.

Laura delivered the trademark smile with an ease that chilled me to my bones. "Yes, it's a simple hit."

From the start of our working relationship, Trident and I had a strict, if unspoken, policy of not directly involving ourselves in local politics, especially when guns were involved. This included no carrying out hits and no sourcing and/or supplying of weapons. We had walked this line pretty successfully until now.

To be honest, everything that happened in the small nation state of Northern Ireland could be linked back to the political situation in one way or another, but we never faced them directly, that would be akin to taking sides and neither of us was keen on doing something crazy like that.

Rather than the "simple hit" Laura suggested, this would need to be a job for the diplomatic, and I don't think either Trident or I had the qualifications, experience, or inclination to carry it off successfully.

Also, there had been rumours of the local paramilitaries wanting Thompsons as "their turf" as far back as I can remember. But support for such groups had been in decline since the signing of the Belfast Agreement in 1998[3]. So, why now? What as to be gained?

Laura point blank refused to give us the targets name until we were sure we were taking the job,

---

[3] also known as the Good Friday Agreement or GFA

but just kept repeating that he was a commander of one of the factions in the immediate local area. It didn't smell right and we all know the golden rule by now, if it feels wrong, it is wrong.

So, naturally, we agreed... but on conditions.

Chapter 7: The Legwork

Portuguese Nights

The night was still,
Disturbed only occasionally,
By Portuguese people,
Going to Portuguese places.

Dave Milliken

17 May 2019

Well, when I say we agreed, a more accurate description would be that Trident agreed. I managed to add the caveat that our current level of agreement was really just that we would look into it, think about it, and get back to her. But this wasn't ideal either. The fact we were considering it could be trouble enough.

If the word got out that Trident and I were taking local jobs, either deliberately from Laura, her man-mountain of a PA/bodyguard/statue, or through some other leaky mechanism, noses could be put out of joint, targets would be placed on people's backs, and excrement would start hitting physically rotational cooling devices. Our reputations for being 'impartial' would be destroyed and we would probably never be able to work here again as free agents.

But we were where we were and it was what it was.

Back at the safehouse we busied ourselves, packing away our equipment and cleaning the place down. We worked methodically and in silence, each respectful of each other's quiet time. We had the place stripped and decontaminated within the hour.

It was shortly after 2000hrs that the landlady showed up for the final inspection. She knocked politely on the already ajar door and let it swing open to announce her arrival. Trident swung into action with his performance.

"Rita, how lovely to see you again.", his usually deadpan voice taking on a little more character. Rita, a thin woman about 5 foot tall with large round gold-rimmed glasses and her greying brown hair in a super tight pony tail, who looked like a deer stuck in headlights at the best of times, almost froze in place from the warmth and enthusiasm of Trident's greeting. Trident strode forward and, ignoring Rita's outstretched hand, enveloped her in a tight embrace. "We are just about finished here", continuing with his arm around her shoulders and guiding her deeper into the room, almost against her will. We had finished nearly an hour and a half ago.

Although nervous, Rita cast a critical eye around the room, looking for things that were out of place, or something that might involve an additional charge. But if she did see anything, she said nothing. "Did... did you enjoy your stay?" she stammered.

"We did, didn't we, Jack?" Trident beamed and cast a look over his shoulder at me, not really expecting a reply. Jack was my alias for this job. "Jack doesn't say much, but were really enjoyed our time here. Do you do offer frequent visitor discounts?" This was followed by a wholesome, hearty laugh to punctuate the joke. Rita's face barely broke a smile.

Rita, struck by the onslaught of engagement, tried to reclaim control of the situation. "And the fancy locks and door, will you be returning them to what we had previously?"

"Rita," Trident clasped the slight lady's shoulders in each hand and lowering himself to her eye level, "those are our gift to you!" And with that, he fished into his pocket and retrieved a set of keys and codes need to open and reset the lock on the door and pressed them into Rita's hand.

Rita was visibly shocked. "Oh! Thank you?" was all she managed, breaking eye contact with Trident and looking down at her hands.

Trident made an obvious check of his watch, "Well, Rita, as much as I would love to, we can't stand around chatting all day, we have a plane to catch. Come along, Jack. We must be off." With that, he disengaged from Rita's emotional space and walked straight out the door. I grabbed a final cavass bag of uneaten [4]MRE's and followed, smiling meekly at Rita and silently mouthing the words "Thank you", as I left.

---

[4] MRE: Meal, Ready-to-Eat – usually used by the military to feed their troops in the field.

As we drove away, Trident in the driver seat, I couldn't help but smile. "You enjoyed that, didn't you?".

A wry smile played on Tridents lips "Maybe just a little."

It was, at last, starting to get dark.

It was a one-hour drive back to our main accommodation. Located far enough from major cities and towns to be difficult to find for anyone not familiar with the area. But it was close enough that few places would take more than a couple of hours to get to. A barn that had been turned into an open plan living space; it served our purpose well.

A large, warm communal space for the usuals of daily living, living area, kitchen, small gym. But also provided private living quarters at opposing ends of the building. A sleeping area, toilet/showering facilities, and a small reception for entertaining. Not that we got much time to entertain, all we seemed to do was work.

The barn itself, and the land it sat on, were owned by an old friend of Trident, Gusty Burke. Gusty was a man who had made his fortune in the shady, cutthroat world of politics and high finance. It was he who we were going to speak with first.

For most people over 60, the hours post 2200hrs were for tv shows, putting your feet up, and winding down after a long day of being old. But not for Gusty. As soon as we had arrived home, Trident insisted we speak with him right away. And, upon knocking on the double wooden doors of the large manor house that sat not 200 metres from our barn, we had been ushered inside by the house keeper, led to a lounge, and offered refreshments. I had only ever been in here once before and that was when we were signing our rental agreement. It truly was a relic from the previous century. Or was it the century before that? High ceilings with ornate light fittings surrounded by plaster rose decorations, tall windows that maintained the overall antiquated feel of the property but also afforded the luxury of aircon and maximise privacy, and deep carpets that made walking around the property feel like walking on clouds of slightly different textures.

The lounge, or drawing room, or whatever, was tactfully furnished with fixtures from whatever century this was supposed to represent. Shelves of paper books, the really old kind with leather covers, wooden roman blinds, and oversized, plush, wing-backed armchairs made me nervous about touching anything. In my hand, I cradled a glass of, what I am reliably told was, 3-fingers of 30-year-old whiskey that had been matured on these very premises. I didn't know about that, but all whiskey tasted the same to me... terrible.

Before entry, Trident had warned me, as he had on the day of the lease signing, not to speak until we were in the company of Gusty. There would be listening and recording devices all over the home, so not saying anything whilst not in Gusty's presence would prevent us from saying anything that might be taking out of context or cause offence without the opportunity to repair the damage. Respect, or at least Gusty's understanding and interpretation of the word respect, was very important within these walls, and could come with dire and immediate consequences.

Trident sipped his whiskey, looking appreciatively at the glass after each taste. Trident had the taste for such things, but I wasn't sure if this was theatre for some unseen observer. Whiskey was still awful.

As I glanced casually around the room, hoping to see the telltale flashing red light of the hidden camera when the house keeper returned.

The housekeeper, a short woman, perhaps in her 60's, carrying a bit of extra weight, and with a motherly attitude, announced that Mr Burke would see us now, and bid that we follow her. Moving through the corridors at an alarming speed, Trident and I almost had to break into a jog to keep up. But after a minute or two of traversing hallways and stairs filled with expensive looking paintings of people who were probably long dead, and large free-standing clocks that made very loud and annoying noises every hour, on the hour, we were finally led into a very dark room. My light compensators kicked in.

The room was spacious and long, and held 4 full size pool tables generously positioned. Above each hung enclosed florescent tube lighting, concentrating the light exclusively upon the table it hung above. Each wall was lined with pool cues, some of varying lengths and styles, and each table had its own scoring plaque, complete with adjustable hands to indicate how many games each player had won. All the tables were occupied by at least 2 players.

Gusty, a man with an aging athlete's body and thinning grey hair on his head, stood in a casual grey suit with a pool cue in his hand, patiently waiting for his opponent to take their shot.

"Trident." He said, offering his hand to my friend who shook it with full eye contact and a deliberate, but almost imperceivable, nod. "And you, ", he pointed the open hand at me ", I have forgotten your name."

"My name is Blades, sir.", and I shook his hand too.

"Trident and Blades, huh?" He mused. "Boys, they are possibly the stupidest names I have ever heard." He mocked, and the other players laughed. And then, screwing up his face in mock puzzlement, he asked, "And you picked these names for yourselves?"

Trident smiled and laughed, obviously in on the joke, "They get 'assigned' to you over time, Gusty, you know that. Trident was my military callsign." Gusty smiled and nodded.

"And what about your name, son?" He asked.

"Oh, I have, er, had ", I cast a fleeting nervous glance at Trident, who was still smiling "a proclivity with knives and other bladed weapons, sir." There was a low wave of laughter that rolled through the room, the elders in attendance clearly finding this amusing.

Gusty feigned surprise, "Oh? And what about now, Blades?"

Again, I glanced at Trident, for nothing other than a bit of moral support, "Well, I still like them, sir, but I have had to upskill in recent years."

"And why was that, boy?" A new voice entered the conversation, sharper, crisper, and more demanding than the previous. I couldn't immediately identify the source.

"Because you can't run with the big dogs if you still piss like a puppy." I replied with almost child-like honesty.

The entire room erupted in to laughter, and Gusty slapped his hand down hard on my shoulder. "Truer words were never spoken, my good friend, Blades."

We spoke for several hours. Trident and I outlined the situation, our execution of the Quigley job (which felt like a lifetime away now), our unofficial "don't get involved in local politics" policy, and the position we now found ourselves in with Laura and her hit. Gusty was very intrigued and more than a bit entertained by our predicament. But he listened. Only chiming in to ask a question or seek clarification on one point or another.

"Well, boys ", he said once we were all talked out, "You might have to leave that one with me for a couple of days. I can ask around. You may just have struck lucky, this doesn't sound like a move by the local militia, to me. This sounds like plain old greed by a small-time commander who is getting too big for his britches."

Trident nodded his head, "We would appreciate any information you can give us, Gusty.

But tonight, we have taken up far too much of your time, thank you for being so patient. Just give us a shout when you hear back from your sources." Trident shook Gusty's hand.

I reached out my hand. "Thank you for your time, Mr Burke."

He looked me in the eye, and with the shadow of a smile on his lips, he shook it in a firm grip and said, "Call me Burkie."

Chapter 8: Toys, Toys, Toys.

Existential Dread

I want to sink my head,
Pretend I was dead,
Need to get away,
From this existential dread.

Dave Milliken

28 September 2021

It had been a wild week. The Quigley hit, the meet with Laura, and then, finally, last night's meet with Burkie.

The meeting with Burkie didn't make a lot of sense. But then, a lot of what was happening didn't make a lot of sense to me. I have very little doubt that, in whatever ego-induced, chemically-assisted haze this guy lived in, claiming Thompsons Garage for his clan was the right next move for his career. The fact that he would probably draw the ire of every other commander within a 10-mile radius would probably never even factor into his battle calculus.

For the uninitiated, it broadly worked like this. Belfast was split, not just into the cardinal points, although that was important too, it was split by 'area'. The area you lived in was control by a local, independent paramilitary organisation. These groups would, of course, be part of a much larger group, but would take care of the day-to-day stuff, like terrorising their natives and raising funds (ironically, by terrorising their natives). This could happen directly through intimidation or indirectly through propaganda and controlling the narrative.

The larger group would have the lofty overall vision, goal, and strategy, for example, the reunification of Ireland or killing all of one particular religion or another, and the smaller local groups would act broadly in accordance with achieving these objectives.

Each area had a commander, or whatever (depending on the organisation, this position could be named differently), and it was their job to recruit members, maintain discipline, manage training, and work towards the overarching goal of their particular organisation, often with the, not too gentle, guidance from the organisations higher command. This meant that the commanders were always top dog within their own area, but were often at odds with the poor, disrespectful treatment they faced from their higher ups. As a result of this, the occasions of coups, internal conflict, defections, and just general discontentment were frequent and often very violent. The commander in vogue today, could be dead in a ditch tomorrow. So, you can see the structure is very much one that started in the military realm (most of these organisations started as military units of one type or another at the time they went rogue), and have taken on a more extreme form of middle management passive aggressiveness, with a lethargy being applied to the passivity and an emphasis on the aggression.

This is why I refused to work with them, not some misplaced sense of morality. Money was money, and, to be fair to them, they had a reputation for usually paying well and paying promptly.

But it could get messy, very quickly, and you never really knew who you were working for, or what fallout would come from who you were working against. It just didn't make good sustainable business sense.

But, in the plus column, I was finally getting my toy today.

In a mall called Forestside, just on the fringes of Belfast city, was a rack of Click and Collect lockers. And in locker number 47 was box advertising the Nerf Elite 2. It was heavier than you would expect a toy made of plastic to be and came with a backpack of spare magazines, sound suppressor, and a laser sight. I cooly doffed the bag, a support over each shoulder, and adjusted the straps for comfort and stability. After a visual inspection of the box, assessing it for its structural integrity, I didn't want to lift it only for its true contents to come tumbling out, I tucked it under my left arm, closed the locker, and headed to the car. It was reassuringly heavy and I struggled to contain my excitement. Looks like we were going to the range tomorrow.

As I made my way through the mall, even offering a cheeky nod to one of their armed security guards, I called Trident through my implanted radio.

"It arrived.", I said.

I could hear the excitement rise in Trident's voice, "Just got a message myself. I am going pick them up on the way home. Shall I book the range for tomorrow morning?"

"Absolutely!" I hung up. The complexities and worries of the past couple of days melted away with the knowledge that tomorrow we were going shooting.

***

It was 0532hrs the next morning. I know this because Trident took every opportunity to remind me, between large gulps of coffee and over exaggerated yawns.

The only sound from my electric car was a light whine and you could hear the satisfying crunch of rubber wheels on gravel as we rolled to a halt in front of the shooting range. There was another car in the gravel drive that also served as the carpark, so we had a good idea that Cool Hand Luke was already here.

Contrary to popular belief, while there were several restrictions and a robust registration process, firearms, in general, were not illegal in Northern Ireland, or the broader United Kingdom, for that matter. Any firearm under a certain length were definitely illegal, but you could get around this by adding a stock and/or an extended muzzle (sound suppressors were also not illegal). There were shooting clubs, not just for shotguns, where you could go and practice, legally. Now, I wouldn't go so far as to say that Trident and I had a lovely collection of legally approved and registered firearms, certainly not. But we had a contact who owned and ran one of these clubs, and if we came really early, and picked up all our spent brass, he would let us use his ranges.

A pet peeve for me, who had been working the more shadowy job market for the past 3 or four years, was the skill and discipline levels in the pool of people available for me to work with. Many of these guys had never even been given competent instruction on how to fire a weapon, so there was absolutely no understanding of safe practice such as muzzle or trigger control, or even how to clean and maintain their weapons. Placing you and the rest of their team in just as much danger as the people they were shooting at. The vast majority of the employment pool would be perfectly comfortable getting drunk and/or high before a job, standing in the open, firing their weapon, single-handed, in the general direction of their target, all while shouting "Yippy Ki-Yay". No, these were clowns that I did not want to partner up with. Trident, on the other hand, was highly trained and very disciplined. His military experience and habits were still sharp. We would try to get the range at least once a month, and make a point of cleaning and oiling the tools of our trade before and after each visit, regardless if they were discharged.

Having access to the range was a great opportunity to try out the new ADS Amphibious assault rifle I purchased from Laura.

The range itself consisted of a couple of fields, a main building with an indoor range, and a barn that had been converted into a configurable 'kill house'. I stepped from the car and made my way to the boot as Trident got out and started towards to the main building. Retrieving the heavy, oversized, black, canvass bag, I shouldered it and hurried to catch up. We reached the front entrance together, a set of double doors sporting reinforced windows embedded in the top half and peeling light green paint. They look like they had been stolen from my high school. Seeing the door was unlocked, I made my way in calling Lukes's name. Trident, secured the doors behind us.

"I'm in here." A voice responded from an office just behind the main reception. As you came in the front doors, there was a reception desk hollowed out in the left-hand wall consisting mostly of a countertop and liftable hatch. This was where members would sign in before following the corridor another 10 metres or so to the actual range. Behind the reception was the door to the office.

The office took up all the space behind the corridor wall and was linked directly to the range. In fact, half the office was made up of a couple of desks, bookshelves, and filing cabinets etc., while the other half had firearms cabinets, miscellaneous weapons parts, and ammunition stores. There was a countertop that separated the store from the range, much like at the reception, and offered a kind of barrier between guests and the guns and ammunition they desired.

I exchanged glances with Trident, before making my way to the office, struggling to get the oversized bag through the narrow gap of the hatch and the office doorway.

Luke was sitting behind a desk that was covered with miscellaneous paperwork, unidentifiable gun parts, and a massive mug of coffee. He was wearing a blue plaid shirt, navy blue work trousers, complete with kneepad inserts, and brown Timberland boots.

Luke had an uncanny way of looking at you like he had never laid eyes upon you before. Like I said previously, we were here at least once every month and had been for the last 18 months, so I always found this really disconcerting. The best I could say for him was that he was average. Average height, average build, average weight (although maybe a little above average on this one), but keenly intelligent and was a little more unique these days with his red lumberjack hair and beard.

"You are late." He said, drinking from the oversized cup that sported the phrase "World's Best Dad" in large, black words, using a font that was giving me a headache.

Trident looked at his watch and sighed, "We are 10 minutes early, Luke!"

Luke brightened up immediately, "You are right! So, what do you think? Should we use the indoor or outdoor range today?"

"Indoor might be best?", I offered, more as a question than a statement.

"Oh!", Luke replied, his eyebrows raised high on his forehead, "Do you have a new toy?"

I smiled, "I do."

"Well, let's stop yakking and get to it." He pushed his chair away from his desk, stood up, and made his way to the store room half of the office.

Standing between us and the assortment of weapons, accessories, and ammunition in the store, Luke turned and signalled for us to stop "Sorry, guys. But I can't let you go any further without proving to me you know your firearm safety protocol. We have to do it. What are the safety rules of handling firearms."

Without missing a beat, Trident and I began to recite the rules of firearm safety, in the dull monotone chorus of people in a restaurant singing happy birthday to someone they didn't really like, as we had done many, many times before.

"1. Treat every firearm like it is loaded. 2. Don't point your firearm at anything you aren't willing to kill or destroy. 3. Don't put your finger on the trigger until you are willing to kill or destroy that thing. 4. Muzzle discipline is not just a safety rule, it is a sign of respect."

Luke listened intently, "And if we need to pass a weapon to our buddy, how do we do it?"

"Butt first, beach open, chamber and magazine well empty." Came our reply.

Luke nodded in satisfaction. "You know, you would think you guys had said that before. Right," he clapped his hands, rubbing them together in excitement and anticipation, "let's get started."

After 20 minutes or so of painstakingly selecting the right ammunition and filling some magazines with the selected rounds, Luke turned to us with an apologetic look on his face.

"Semi-auto only today, boys."

I am not sure if they are haunted by the lost souls taken by the members who frequent the club or what, but every shooting range I have been to, regardless of this location, has been freezing cold in the morning. It is no normal cold either. It is that cold that reaches through your skin, into your bones, right into your spiritual core. We had taken some time to look over and lovingly admire our new toys, strip them down and examine their inners, not just for safety reasons either, but out of genuine interest. Luke suggested that this might have been the first rifle he had seen designed for underwater engagements, then modified to improve accuracy out of the water. Apparently, it usually happened the other way around. And finally, after testing and zeroing our new accessories, we put up some fresh target sheets and had some fun.

When it came to firearms, no one came close to Trident's cool, calm, precision. Every movement refined, every procedure drilled to almost perfection. And the most disturbing thing was that he could do it under the intense pressure of being under fire too. I had seen it. There is something unnerving about watching someone clear a breach after a misfire, all whilst incoming rounds pinged the ground and walls around him. And then there was his accuracy...

We spent the greater part of the morning there, Luke warning us that we were good up until around 0830hrs, when the regular members would start showing up.

Despite the range being remote, all the neighbours were farms, so firing rounds at 0500hrs would not be waking anyone up. Luke stressed again that we needed to keep the fire modes at semi-automatic. His neighbours were understanding, they were not idiots.

But the general feel of the visit was one of satisfaction. Laura had done well. The weapons and their accessories had outperformed our expectations, and while we could not confirm that the burst or full-auto modes would work, after Luke's inspections of their mechanisms, in theory at least, it appeared everything should work as advertised.

By 0800hrs and about 500 rounds of ammunition placed down range between the three of us, we had broken down, cleaned, and oiled the guns, before reassembling them, placing them back in the canvass bag, then stowed them in the trunk of the car. We returned to the office for a coffee with Luke.

"So, how is work with you boys?" Luke knew what we did and while I don't think he agreed with the morals of our profession, I think he respected our professional attitude to the tools of our trade and the fact that we mostly tried to avoid collateral damage.

The definition of collateral damage can be very subjective.

"Good," I said, around a chocolate biscuit. "We are actually between jobs right now. That is why we took some time to re-equip".

Luke nodded, maintaining contemplative eye contact, "Is the MP5 still giving you bother?"

"Yeah, the charging handle was still a bit hit and miss. You remember, it would slide forward in a light breeze. I thought it might be an apt time to replace it." Luke had done some work on it, tightening it up as much as possible without interfering with the action. But it was old, and the metal that held the charging handle back was had just worn away of the years of use. The simplest solution would be some welding, but that would involve getting someone else in and the risk and cost just weren't worth it.

"You know, if you were looking to move it on, let me know, I would be interested in, maybe, providing it a new home."

I paused "Sure, I will think about it", before finishing the biscuit and reaching for my coffee. I could feel Trident imploring me not to look at him. This was very out of character. Luke was as straight as they come, you had to be to be allowed to run a place like this. It was out of some form of brother-in-arms comradery, that a civvy like me would never understand, Cool Hand Luke would flaunt, and maybe occasionally break the rules for Trident. But the idea that Luke would actually want to own something as illegal as an H&K MP5 submachine gun, well, that wasn't just weird, that was a serious red flag.

Tridents phone rang.

Chapter 9: The Ugly Truth

Look at these sewer rats,
They never stop dying for me.

Dave Milliken

15 June 2023

On the car journey back home, I asked Trident about his relationship with Luke. Luke worked in deactivating landmines while he was out East and, despite the fact that he ran a gun club and shooting range, really had little interest in owning guns himself. He didn't need to. With the connections he would make from his members, who were rumoured to show up with all forms of heavy metal and ammunition, Luke would have the opportunity to fire many different types of weapons, legal and otherwise, without ever having to risk keeping one on the premises. No, this was a worrying development.

Trident's phone call had been from Burkie. He had dug up some information and was inviting us back to the manor to discuss it. It was barely passed 0900hrs, and as I had said before, Burkie was a night owl, so it must be important that it couldn't wait.

We once again stood in the dark pool hall, I felt just as awkward as I did the previous time. Gusty, er, I mean, Burkie stood in a light grey 3-piece that would have almost looked comical if we had been anywhere else but here. He was holding his pool cue, waiting patiently to take his shot. Once again, all the pool tables were occupied, there was very little chatter, and the only ambient noise was of pool balls colliding, sometimes with the occasional satisfying thud as a ball was potted followed by the sound of it making its way through the pools tables digestive system to finally take up residence in the glass fronted display on the side of the table along with all the other potted balls.

"You boys get up early, don't you?" Burkie said, studying the table like a chess master getting ready to close down and check a lesser experienced opponent. Burkie leaned across the table and started to line up his shot.

"We had some biz out of the city, Burkie. And young Blades here, likes to get up with the birds." Trident was careful not to interfere with the shot about to be taken.

"I see, ", Burkie paused from his shot and without disturbing his hand configuration on the table, looked up at Trident, "so how is Cool Hand Luke?"

Trident, smiled, "He is very well. I didn't realise you two were friends?"

"Uh huh. I didn't realise I needed to run it past you." Burkie said sharply, returning to his shot, but then softened his tone a little. "Maybe 'friend' is too strong a word, but in our line of work, he is an important acquaintance to have. I figured you boys would pay him a visit after you had spoken with your friend... "He pointed at me after sinking his shot and taking an extra moment to remember her name "...Laura."

"How well do you know Laura, Mr Blades?"

"Oh, ", I was a bit shocked and unprepared to have the question, especially this question, posed to me. "I guess I've known her for a couple of years."

"You guess?" Burkie responded, now standing again and with, what I assumed was, a glass of whiskey. I glanced to Trident who, I now realised, was also cradling a glass of whiskey in his hands. It was barely 0930hrs in the morning!

Again, I felt totally out of my depth, "I mean, I have known her for a couple of years, we dated for part of that but then decided to just be friends."

"Who decided that you should just be friends?"

"Well, me, I guess, I mean, I know. I was the one who broke it off." I corrected myself.

"I see," Burkie gave a nod of approval for my correction and newly found assertiveness. "And the bump, was that your doing?"

"Oh no! She said she went to the clinic for that."

"You don't think she could be setting you up? You know what they say about a woman scorned."

I thought for a moment, "No, that really isn't her style. And if she really did want revenge, I have absolutely no doubt that I would be dead by now."

"Hmm, it is all looking a bit messy, boys." Burkie took his next shot, missing the pocket. "Have either of you two ever heard of the company, 'Big Idea'?" We both nodded, it was a locally recognised company, pretty much a household name, that offered market research campaigns, if my memory served me correctly. It was virtually impossible to move through Belfast without seeing some form of advertisement of their services. "Well, I think we have good news and bad news."

Big Idea had been nothing but a small start-up not 2 years ago. But with the right people on their side, and a number of regional government contracts, they had grown in size considerably. I kept as much of an eye on the corporate world as I had too, for the purposes of finding work, but

Big Idea would not let me ignore them. We had never worked for them, but I had expressed an interest in a job or two in the past. Nothing ever really serious. Minor stuff like "find this guy's mistress and tell us her dogs name", or "go cause some trouble over there, at this time, for this duration." All pretty pedestrian, and all weirdly exact. But Big Idea worked primarily in conducting customer and market research with side gigs in software development.

Burkie continued, "The good news is that your political hymen is still intact. This move was not sanctioned by any paramilitary I, or any of my associates, know of, so you can take that word as gospel.

"The bad news is that when I looked a little deeper, and not much deeper, by the way, I discovered something else and it involves this company Big Idea. They are looking to burst onto the global stage and in a big way."

"What could a company that carries out customer service surveys want with the likes of a paramilitary commander?", I pondered out loud.

"Exactly!" Burkie, potted another ball, clearly signalling the end of their game and the ending of our conversation.

"So, what is the motive?" Trident asked.

Burkie's opponent, a well-known, yet reformed, ex-paramilitary enforcer spoke. "In my humble opinion, sounds like a simple and traditional intimidation job. Commander puts pressure on Laura to become part of his turf and if she doesn't, they will cause her all sorts of havoc. She can't go to the authorities, given that she has been effectively running an illegal rave for the past 50 years, not to mention her arms dealing on the side.

"If she goes to the other local commanders, they will all be wanting some form of quid pro quo.

"Then, out of the blue, comes this benevolent corporation called Big Idea, who is willing to help a single mother in her time of need by offering to buy out Thompsons Garage at a fraction of its true worth, miles below market value, but still giving Laura enough that she and her foetus can live out the remainder of their lives in reasonable luxury. And Big Idea get some prime Belfast City Centre real estate for a serious knock down price, all in time for their global launch."

"Do you want a second opinion?" Burkie asked.

"Sure!"

"You're also ugly!"

More laughter.

Chapter 10: Don't Run with the Big Dogs

Sometimes

Sometimes, I forget just how alone I really am.

Dave Milliken

18 June 2023

Once back at the barn, I stowed the weapons in a wall safe and prepared a coffee. Trident had headed off on some personal errand so I had some to think for myself. So, with my coffee, I took a seat in the lounge area and watched the rain come down in sheets through the floor to ceiling window and let my mind ponder.

It had been a couple of days since we spoke with Laura and I was keen to get back to her as soon as possible to let her know one way or the other. In many ways, it was quite a relief to hear that there was no support from the paramilitary command structures, on either side of the political divide, for the move on Thompsons. Burkie might even had hinted that some of the leadership elements might even be against the idea. And it was also kind of reassuring that there was a corporation behind it. Just business as usual.

I guess whoever was heading up Big Idea didn't fully understand the possible knock-on consequences of invoking paramilitary assistance and the civil instability it could bring to the area. Although, I couldn't help but think that was a ruse. Whether it was the commander or their contact at Big Idea who came up with it, it was a really short-sighted scheme and could even lead to a full-scale, yet localised, conflict that could last years, even decades. I was not even convinced that removing the commander would fix the problem. Big Idea could just find someone else with questionable morals and a hungry bank balance to start the intimidation project all over again. And these days, those are a dime a dozen. Meanwhile, Thompsons garage loses the support of those who believe the rumours, and burn through any favours they may be owed.

But it made sense that a ham-fisted corporate executive, with no understanding of the local politics or culture, would think that this was a good idea. Drive the price of property down to basement level, then buy, buy, buy. And then, just wait for the internal promotions or job offers from rival firms to roll in. And the best way to do this was through the infrastructure that already existed. An even mix of overconfidence and arrogance have become so apparent that I could almost smell the pretentious Gucci cologne that the executive undoubtably wore.

I was starting to think that another meeting with Laura, a more honest and direct chat should be on the cards. I think if we compared notes, we might be able to join some dots. But, as I mentioned earlier, arms dealers are notoriously paranoid. I sent a message asking for another face to face.

Trident returned an hour later. I explained my thinking and he nodded his agreement as he listened. If we could at least check for consistencies between Burkie's intel on Big Idea and Laura's concerns about the commander, we could at least have an idea of what to expect in the aftermath or if things go pear-shaped.

Trident agreed, we could take out the commander, but someone else would take the job. But he also came with a hard truth. I might be letting my feelings for Laura cloud my judgement.

This was a job, like any of the dozens we had done over the past 18 months. We were being asked to delete someone, nothing more, nothing less. We had done this before. And, yes, it was wise to make sure that everything was as it seemed. But at the end of the day, all we had to do was kill, what amounted to be, an overzealous local thug. Now we knew that he was acting out of school, and there would be little or no response to his assassination, we had the green light. If Big Idea decides to hire someone else, and Laura has the money, we will kill them too. It was not our place to get involved. He was right. I had let my emotions get the better of me. But, as a form of consolation, Trident still agreed that a face to face with Laura would be a good idea.

Chapter 11: Big Trouble

Blank like an A4 sheet,
Kneeling on your throne,
And bleat like a sheep,
The wolf is near,
But all that remains is fear.

Dave Milliken
17 March 2023

I checked my watch for the fifth time. She was late and that was not normal. Trident took a bite from his croissant and paused before chewing. He looked me in the eye and, with a stern expression on his face that suggested "you are getting on my nerves", said "She will be here."

"I know, I know." I replied, taking a sip of my latte. But I didn't know. And as much as our romance was water under the bridge, I still cared a great deal for her. If Laura was anything, it was that she was punctual.

We were sitting in the Breakfast Shack diner enjoying some coffee and pastries. It was quiet, a middle of the day loll, and I didn't really know any of the staff on shift but my face was familiar enough to ensure we got space to talk. I almost looked at my watch again but caught myself mid action, much to the chagrin of Trident.

My fears were proved unfounded when an oversized black SUV, with darkened windows pulled up outside. From the front passenger side stepped the familiar bulk of Steve, the 'personal assistant', wearing the narrowest, most ridiculous dark glasses you could imagine. He moved to the rear passenger side door and, giving a quick look around, opened it and with great care and attention, helped Laura debus before closing it again. Laura looked dwarfed by the massive vehicle, but it was providing amazing body cover against anyone who might want to do her harm. With the same care, Steve the PA walked her up to the diner's front door and, once she was safely inside, stationed himself right in front of it. The Breakfast Shack was effectively closed for the duration of our meeting.

I got up and helped Laura, who was now wearing a black dress and grey blazer, into the bench seat beside Trident. Her bump seemed even bigger now. A server quickly appeared and took Laura's order for an ice tea. It appeared almost instantly. I couldn't help but start to think that someone had called ahead to ensure our meeting had some privacy.

Retaking my seat, I address Laura directly, as she sipped her ice tea through the metal straw she had taken from her bag.

"Who is the commander, Laura?"

She paused, "Does that mean you are taking the job?"

"Yes, we are." Trident interjected, "Who is the commander?"

Laura smiled a broad smile, relief washing over her. "Tucker Boyd. Do you know him?" She glanced between us.

"I do." I replied, joining Laura in the relief. "He is universally hated by virtually everyone, but perhaps most by his own people."

"What do you know about Big Idea?" Trident pushed on, trying to keep the momentum of the conversation.

Laura looked genuinely confused. "Big Idea? What have they got to do with this?"

I gave Trident a silent, but sincere, look of thanks. "We think it was Big Idea who hired Boyd to start the threats. As far as we can ascertain, there has been no order from any paramilitary organisation to add Thompsons Garage to their turf."

Laura sat back and rubbed her pregnant belly. She sighed. "Big Idea have been pretty aggressive in trying to buy Thompsons. I've had 3 offers from them in the last month alone. All lowballing it, mind you." It was clearly all clicking into place for her. "So, it really doesn't matter if we remove Boyd, does it?"

"Oh no, we are going to eliminate Boyd, and for the price we agreed on. I know him too, and you will be doing the world a service. But what you need to think about is how to get Big Idea off your back. Who has been making the offers?"

"Yeah, that was weird. An American woman called Boyard, Megan Boyard, I think. But she was from their public relations department. She was really insistent, and I kept thinking, why are the public relations department trying to buy my bar?"

"Big Idea have plans to go global in the next couple of months. They want some city centre real estate to operate from." I said.

Laura started to giggle "Really? All this for some real estate? I have an old warehouse, not half a km from Thompsons that they could have had for a steal. I am sick of paying rates for a building that I no longer have any use for."

"Oh!", I said brightly, "Then the problem is solved. Give Big Idea a ring tomorrow and let them know that the warehouse is on the market."

Laura fixed me with the most patronising of stares, making me feel really quite small. "Oh, Johnathan. If only things were so simple." She smiled her trademark smile and my blood ran cold.

Two days later, I sat in the Big Idea offices, feeling very out of place in my suit and tie, and completely naked without my pistol. Trident had encouraged me to leave it behind. It was a good job too because the two buff security guards, whilst being incredibly polite, even apologetic, were extraordinarily robust in their full body pat down, and that was just getting through the front door. I would imagine they had any number of less visible weapon detection devices to catch what their physical security might had missed.

We had managed to get a meeting with Boyard at their offices in an industrial estate on the fringe of Belfast, called Boucher, posing as a real estate magnate and possible investor.

I was sitting in a foyer that was impossibly clean. Lots of glass and steel illuminated with low intensity lighting. It gave the place a feel of calm while I drank my professionally prepared flat white. The receptionist looked more like any receptionist that I had ever seen and may, indeed, have been the mould from which all other receptionists were formed.

After about 5 minutes, the console on the reception desk beeped and I was told to make my way down the hallway to conference room 3. Under the watchful eye of the receptionist, I did as I was told, following the instructions to the letter, and resisting all temptation to go exploring by myself. It wasn't every day I found myself in such a privileged and lucrative position. Upon reaching the door, I knocked politely.

The door was opened and I was greeted by a tall blonde woman. Much like the receptionist, Megan Boyard was exactly what you would imagine some who worked in PR would look like. Tall, slender, blonde hair, blue eyes, 30 something, with shapes where shapes should be. But, unlike the receptionist and the security guards, she carried the awkwardness and palpable insecurity of someone who felt they may be fired at any moment.

She smiled, a broad, warm smile but with eyes who had no invite to the party. "Come in, Mr Hughes. Take a seat." She took a couple of steps back into the room and motioned to a pair of plush office chairs in front of a desk. On the wall was the projected image of Big Idea, a thought bubble with the words 'Big Idea' written inside it. As I passed her on my way into the room, I smelled the Gucci cologne – called it!

"Good morning, Ms. Boyard? Thank you for seeing me on such short notice."

"Please, call me Megan." Her smile widened for an instant. "And it was a pleasure to be able to fit you in today."

"Very well, Megan, you can me Johnathan." The words were out of my mouth before I could stop them. It probably wasn't a good idea to share your real first name, even in such an asinine situation as this, with someone who may be interviewed by the authorities in the near future. But it was already done. To my horror, she wrote it down as well.

For the next hour we spoke about investment opportunities and projected plans of the company. Every time she said my name, and it was a lot, I winced internally. There was no mention of going global or floating on the stock exchange, or anything like that. Just talk about their strategies for building new and developing current business accounts. I have to hand it to her, if I had the money, I probably would have invested.

Before I left, she insured that I had taken a business card with her personal number, written in blue ink, included on the back. I should call her anytime, day or night, with any questions I might have.

Trident listened carefully as I retold the conversation with Megan Boyard earlier that morning. "What do you think Laura will do?" He asked.

"Honestly, I imagine she will probably flatten Big Idea, and I mean that literally. Now she knows who is behind the plot, she will be looking to make a statement."

"And what do you know of Boyd?"

"Just what I said yesterday. He is a really horrible piece of work. If we had some time, I am sure we could probably engineer his execution by one of his own." I answered.

"Now that is an interesting thought. So, you know who is next in line?"

"Yeah, his brother Jason. There is a whole clan of them, but I am pretty sure that he would be next in the order of ascension."

"How do you feel about doing this one yourself?" Trident was staring off into the middle distance "You know the Donegall Pass, we would draw too much attention going in together."

"Let me just make some calls and find out exactly where he is." I answered, reaching for our burner phone.

Chapter 12: Things Come to Pass

Alone,
Alone, yet in the zone,
To know is to do,
But nothing depends on you.

Dave Milliken

17 March 2023

It was dark and I was wearing my usual armoured long coat and a boiler suit over my civvies. I was standing outside the last known location of Tucker Boyd, a traditional Belfast terrace house. The sound of partying and dance music could be heard from the upstairs room out here on the street. I knocked firmly three times upon the door and it opened just shy of a minute later, but I could hear the fussing with locks and bolts the entire time.

"What do you want?" Spat a very white, skin headed teen with more tattoos on his face than teeth in his mouth. The pièce de resistance of the ensemble was a swastika in the centre of his forehead.

"I am looking a bag of green." I answered and held up several notes of currency.

The Nazi teen snatched the money from my gloved hand and snapped "Hold on, wait here..." and as he turned away, I stepped into the house and followed him up the garbage strewn hallway, placing a single, silenced 9mm round into the base of his Hitler-loving skull. His body hit the filthy carpet with barely a sound.

It was a very traditional Belfast terrace house. There were 2 rooms off to the right with a staircase and the kitchen straight ahead. The kitchen was in darkness. The first room on the right was probably the parlour, traditionally used for meeting and greeting fancy guests, so that made the second room the scullery. I advanced quickly up the dark hall, ignoring the closed door of the parlour and heading straight into the scullery. Tucker was sitting on a kitchen chair, a bare single bulb hanging from the centre of the ceiling just above his head, like he had just had a great idea. He was surrounded by black plastic bags of who only knows what, with a needle in his arm and a relaxed smile on his face. Even through his drug fuel haze, he looked almost surprised to see me. He raised his arm to point and tried to speak as I raised my silence pistol and shot him twice in the chest. He jolted with each shot then immediately lay still, making one last low gurgle as his final breath left his body. I took a moment. Even after all this time I still wasn't used to killing in cold blood. I paused only long enough to take a picture of my kill.

I turned to leave only to come face to face with the muzzle of a Glock 19. Until this moment, I hadn't realised that breach looked so big when it was being pointed at you from this angle.

My eyes followed the arm all the way up to the holder's face, to see Jason Boyd standing there, displaying no facial expression, looking at the body of his dead brother with eyes devoid of emotion.

"Give me the gun," he said, in a calm, not-my-first-rodeo, deadpan voice, that, upon reflection, reminded me, in many ways, of Trident. I complied without hesitation. "Did you shoot Fisher too?" I nodded, not really knowing who Fisher was, but there was really no advantage to lying or splitting hairs at this point. He almost laughed. "Get out of here.", he mumbled, lowering his pistol.

"W-Wha...?" I started.

"Get out of here." He growled and pushed me roughly towards the open door and into the hallway.

I didn't need to be told a third time. As I left, stumbling over, what I can only assume was, the body of Fisher as I went, I heard Jason Boyd, the new commander of Donegall Pass C Company, discharge his weapon twice into his brother's body. It would later circulate as a rumour that Tucker had gone crazy and killed Fisher in a psychotic rage. His brother, Jason, had acted quickly to prevent any further meaningless loss of life. The police were never called and it never made the news.

I made my way through the rabbit warren of streets until I reach my hotel on the Dublin Road, stopping only briefly in a alley to tear off my boiler suit and setting it alight. It was mostly paper and it burned really quickly. I had checked myself for signs of blood or brain matter beforehand but appeared to be clean. Not that it mattered in the end, because the reception desk was devoid of humans and used a computer-based automatic check-in instead. Once checked in and verified by the computer, I headed to my room to get cleaned up.

I spent the night in the hotel. Unable to sleep. But it wasn't the constant racket of the natives or the sirens from the emergency services on the streets below that kept me awake, it was the executions of the evening that played on my mind. It was at times like this, that I wondered if I was really cut out for this life after all.

As soon as I had gotten back to the hotel, I had gone through the motions of the clean-up process. The jump suit had proven a real time saver, even though I manage not to get covered in gore. But, after about 20 minutes sleep, I check my watch. 0430hrs. Time for a coffee. I checked out of the hotel and made my way to the Breakfast Shack.

Ben was behind the counter as always. Engaged in overnight cleaning duties, he didn't hear me come in.

"Good morning Ben." I said with all the enthusiasm and innocence of someone who had not just murdered two people in the last 6 hours.

Ben immediate turned around and smiled broadly, offering his closed hand for a fist bump. I completed my half of the transaction. "Good morning, Jack" he responded. "Or, is it good afternoon or good evening?" He smiled. "So, Jack. How is the world of high finance?"

"It's murder." I said without a hint of irony. "Just a coffee, this morning, Ben."

"Coming right up, brother. Grab a seat and I will bring it down to you."

I took my usual seat beside the kitchen door. The smell of the kitchen staff preparing todays pastries and bread was really starting to make me feel hungry, but the images of last night's horror show still hadn't faded enough yet. I was starting to see why some operators in this line of work would get tanked on alcohol or strung out on drugs before a job. But not me, I was too much of a purest. A purest with a half-baked moral code. The worst type.

Ben was a tall, handsome lad, probably cresting about 6 feet, with a rangy build. and a mop of meticulously manicured, dirty blond, hair that sat atop of a standard short back and sides cut. He delivered the coffee and reminded me to give him a shout if I needed a top up.

Well, if nothing else, we had the Laura job completed. It was only then that I had remembered that I had not yet sent the encrypted image to Laura. I broke out my phone and made the transfer. In true Laura-style, she responded almost immediately with payment.

At about 0600hrs and about a million cups of coffee later, Trident pulled up onto the pavement that served as a small, unofficial carpark for the Breakfast Shack. Ben hooked him up with some fancy tea, and he sat down on the bench seat facing me.

"How are you?" He said, over a sip of tea.

"I am grand." I lied. I then proceeded to tell him the whole story, including the bit about being caught off-guard by Jason Boyd and almost having my brains introduced to the light of day.

Trident sucked his teeth, "I am sorry, I should have come with you."

"Do you think they would have let us go if you had been there? No way, we lucked out. We would have had to slaughter everyone in that house instead." I lowered my voice, realising I was speaking a little too loud. I glanced around to see if anyone else had noticed, but the Breakfast Shack was empty. How did this place make any money, I wondered. "No, by some miracle only 2 people, two awful people at that, had to die last night, and, thankfully, one of them wasn't me!"

Trident smiled. "Whatever helps you sleep at night." But he knew it didn't.

Chapter 13: The Not OK Coral

> Let me grow old
> With daemons in my head
> And a devil in my bed
>
> Dave Milliken
> November 2022

It was Trident that first noticed the car pull up across the street. We were just chatting about what we would be getting up to later that day. I was intending to call Laura... again, to replace my pistol and Trident, well I am never sure what Trident gets up to when we have a personal day.

I had just divided the payment for the Tucker job when Trident interrupted me.

"Are you armed?", he snapped.

"Well, no. Didn't you pay attention to the story I told you, not an hour ago?"

"Here," he reached into the right side of his jacket and removed a Berretta 92f that I never even know he carried, "take this." He pulled out 2 magazines and placed them on the table beside it.

"Are you insane?" I said as I snatched them up and tried to conceal them under the table, furiously looking about to ensure no one else saw.

"Maybe, but not right now." He quipped then, getting up from his seat and moving to the counter, and bellowed. "Ben, is there a back way out of here?"

Ben, who was now holding a tablet computer and looking like he was doing a stocktake, glanced up from his work and, seeing Trident draw his Glock 17, as more of a question than a statement, stammered "Um, yeah, through the kitchen?"

"Well go! And take the rest of the kitchen staff with you."

"What? What?" But it was too late, Trident had taken the tablet from him and was dragging him towards the kitchen door.

"Go! Now!" Trident shouted. "And call the cops." He yelled as an afterthought. "Blades! Get behind the counter."

As we moved behind the counter, another car pulled up. It was clear now that this was going to be a hit, and given all the activities of the past week or so, it likely to be a hit on us. Trident was taking inventory of weapons and ammunition.

We had two guns, one for him, a Glock 17 with 52 rounds, and one for me, a Berretta 92f with 46 rounds. It was going to be tight. I knew what he was going to say even before he said it.

"Make every shot count, Blades. Bullets are at a premium."

So much for the single bullet theory, huh, Trident? I thought to myself with good humour, but wouldn't dare voice it.

I smiled, suppressing my sarcastic remark. Trident hated my sarcasm, especially in situations like this.

The first burst of incoming rounds took out the front windows and told us that at least one of our attackers had a fully automatic machine gun. That situation was updated when the rest of their party also opened up with fully automatic machine guns.

We cowered behind the surprisingly well constructed counter as glass and coffee syrup and tea rained down upon us as the Breakfast Shacks impressive display was torn up by the hail of incoming metal and hate. So far, the counter was protecting us from the barrage, but that probably wouldn't last long.

Finally, some good news. There was a lull in the shooting as each of the 6 or so assailants paused to reload. This is a rookie mistake most rookies only make once. We were up from behind the cover as quick as a flash and, taking an extra second to aim, opened fire ourselves. With the current ammunition drought we were experiencing, we picked our shots very carefully.

Aiming exclusively for the centre of the seen mass, I took two of our attackers out of the game, Trident claiming two for himself as well. But just before I could get behind cover again, I took a hit to my left shoulder, spinning me round and sending me crashing into the glass fridges behind us. I yelled out in pain and Trident, staying low, came to my side. The bullets kept coming.

He didn't need to ask where I had been hit as the damage to my armoured long coat was quite clear. On quick inspection, he deduced that the coat had taken the brunt of the damage and the bullet had been deflected. But I still had a shattered left humerus, with damage to the left clavicle and scapula too. He fumbled with my t-shirt, trying to get access to the necklace I wore with a single lozenge of fentanyl citrate encased in a metal brooch. He broke the seal of the brooch and, as calmly as you like, pushed the lozenge into my mouth, placing his hands firm over my lips to ensure I didn't spit it out again. Within seconds the pain began to subside and my left arm just felt weird, but not like it had just taken a bullet.

It was around that time that a fragmentation grenade landed with a dull thud, not a half a metre away from us.

We both lunged for it, Trident getting there first, of course, over my injury addled effort. He threw it back the way it came before taking cover and shielding me in the process. Not two seconds later, it detonated, to the screams of some unfortunate victim.

Great! I thought. They have grenades!

The drugs helped me work through the pain, returning fire when we could. But there were still at least 4 remaining and the drugs, or the ammunition, weren't going to last forever.

Ben had clearly done as Trident had asked. But the siren wails were still too far off in the distance to have any effect on our attackers. Trident popped up again and fired rapidly until the slide of this Glock locked back as he emptied his last magazine. He grabbed the Beretta from my weakened grip and checked how many rounds were left. Breathing heavy, he smiled. "This might be it for us, good chum." The pain was back with vengeance, and I was drifting in and out of consciousness. But the moment was not lost on me.

Just then, the sounds screeching tyre and heavier gun fire interrupted our special moment. But not incoming fire, outgoing fire. Trident stole a look over the embattled counter top. "What the…", was all he said.

The gun fire continued until there was silence. I could just about hear the voices call out, car doors slam, and then screeching tyres as they drove away at high speed. I could hear Trident speak in an urgent, but commanding tone that I had rarely heard from him. But I couldn't make out what he was saying or see who he was saying it too. As I lay there, feeling like I was dying, looking up at the destroyed Breakfast Shack counter and back display, I could hear with enhanced clarity the after-effects of the gun fight. Glass continued to fall, wood seemed to splinter anew, and sound of large appliances falling over, filled my mind. Was this how it felt for Tucker Boyd, or Fisher, or Quigley? My left arm was destroyed, because I wasn't wearing under armour. If I made it through this one, a result in which the jury was definitely still out, I would not make that mistake again.

The last thing I remember was the face of Steve, Laura's personal assistant, looming over me and whispering quiet words of encouragement in a soft, southern Irish, accent. I passed out.

Chapter 14: Sticks and Stones

The world is always against you,
You never stop explaining,
You messed up yet another chance,
You never stop complaining.

Dave Milliken

1 August 2022

It was nearly a week before I got out of the clinic. Despite the UK still having a perfectly good National Health Service, when your complaint is that you have been shot in the shoulder and you may have exchanged fire with an unlawful firearm, you might be better looking to the black clinics of Belfast for your medical care.

Thankfully, I paid a subscription for a service just like this.

In the Cathedral Quarter of Belfast, on the top floor of a budget hotel, was just such a black clinic. I don't know what arrangement they had with the official business. I don't know for how long they had been operating from said hotel. All I knew was that it was a lifesaving arrangement. Regardless of the complexities, I had access to a bed and some of the best medical care money could buy for the guts of 6 days. Even longer, if I had wanted it. But my shoulder, other broken bones, and miscellaneous injuries were almost as good new. Medicine had taken great leaps over the years with the implanting of cyberware and use of nanomachine technology. Very thing still felt a little stiff, but the pain was all but gone and I had the full range of motion.

Trident was parked up and waiting for me as I left the hotel foyer.

"How you feeling?" He asked with genuine concern, as I climbed gingerly into the passenger seat.

"Good. Good." I said, tugging on my seatbelt. "Feeling well rested too. Some of the best sleep I have had in years."

I hadn't seen anyone for the entire time I was in the clinic – no visitors allowed. House rules. Not only does it stop infections, but it also prevents shootouts happening in the make-shift ICU. Even phone calls were frowned upon to avoid the possibility of being located. It made sense, given the sort of people who carried insurance like this. It also meant that I hadn't been updated on how we actually got out of the fire fight. So, I took the time to disconnect and actually rest.

As we drove, Trident filled me in. As it happened, Laura had sent her PA, Steve, to meet with me after she had transferred payment. She had been a little concerned when the rumours of what happened started to circulate. Yes! That soon after the event. So, she sent Steve for 2 reasons. One, to ensure that I actually had done what I was contracted to do, and 2, to make sure I was alright. Making it out of an estate after committing murder was no mean feat.

It had taken an hour or so for Steve to get my last known position and had then also heard that we were under fire at the same time. So, with authorisation from Laura, he and the driver had picked up some heavier weapons from the armoury and come to our rescue. Once the man-mountain showed up with his minigun, our assailants decided to call it a day and bugged out.

My injuries were more dire than Trident's assessment revealed, it turned out. Along with a shattered arm and shoulder, I also had several broken ribs and a punctured lung, and I was suffering massive internal bleeding. Had Laura's people not arrived when they did, I would have been toast. It was Steve who carried me to their SUV while being covered by Trident and the driver. But the bad guys were gone. Apparently, the cops arrived only minutes after we left.

But these were the hazards of the job, and this job came with a lot of hazards.

As soon as we got back to the barn, I headed to my rooms to continue my rest. But my head had not been on the pillow for 5 minutes when my phone chimed. It was a message from Laura. She wanted to meet as soon as possible at Thompsons, because we were not to be trusted on our own. Maybe a bit soon to be making jokes, Laura, I thought.

This time when we showed up at Laura's we were both armed. I wore what remained of my armoured long coat, dark grey gaffer tape sealing up the damage and not doing a bad job at blending in with the coat itself. Under this, I slung my faulty MP5. I needed to replace my pistol. I would hopefully be able to this today as well. Trident also sported his long coat, Glock 17, and full-sized Uzi 9mm.

To say that Laura's security team was unhappy with granting us entry was an understatement. They were already very annoyed at the fact we had parked just outside the dilapidated fence. But, at Laura's insistence, we were allowed through. Given the week we had, possibly at her expense, it was the least she could do.

Once again in her fancy office, we sat and sipped fancy coffees and teas, and made small talk like civilized people. At least until Steve the PA and Mr Driver arrived.

As it happened, Ben had not only called the cops but called Laura as well. At the previous meeting with Laura in the Breakfast Shack, PA Steve had left his card and told Ben to call if he ever felt that anything was amiss. Apparently, being kicked out of your place of work through the backdoor by two-gun totting maniacs counted, in Ben's book anyway, as something being amiss. For his clear and quick thinking, Ben was being looked after with a job at Thompsons as a bar back. I was glad to hear that. To be fair, it was I who had brought the trouble to his door in the first place.

Laura laid her cards on the table. The pressure to sell up from Big Idea had increased after Tuckers retirement. She had it on good authority that it was Megan Boyard who had commissioned and sent the team to the Breakfast Shack, although the reason why still wasn't clear. I spoke openly of my meeting with her. I explained of how she gave off a very unstable vibe but otherwise didn't strike me as someone who was used to commissioning our type of work.

"So, what are we thinking? She is a person out of their depth? Desperate people do desperate things." I said, "Is there anything more dangerous?"

"But to hire and send a 10-man team after two, and please don't take offence at this, small time operators with barely 2 years' experience under their belts? It hardly makes sense." Laura smirked, knowing the light-hearted insult would find its mark.

"Oh! How could we possibly take offence at that?" I said sarcastically, raising a gentle laugh from Laura and her people.

Mr Driver spoke for the first time. "In my opinion, they were all high. And not just on run of the mill street drugs. By the looks of things, they were taking a very heavy synthetic. We found a couple of inhalers after they bugged out." His voice was soft and had a strong local accent. "I've never seen it or anything like it before."

Laura took the opportunity to introduce him. "This is Jamie. He was our head doorman at Thompsons up until his promotion about a month ago. He knows his drugs like he knows his scumbags."

Mr Driver, or Jamie, was a shortish man, about 5 feet 8 inches with a bit of a paunch. He certainly didn't look like the head doorman type, but then, pregnant Laura didn't look like a gun runner who sidelined in the illegal nightclub industry. He cut an interesting figure in his black off-the-rack suit, mirrored aviators, and unlit cigarette hanging from his lips. His brown hair was un-styled and brushed roughly into the side shade. He had that permanent 'just rolled out of bed' look about him.

"If I had at to guess," he continued, "I would say it was an upper. Like, way up." He emphasised his point by doing an upward motion with both his thumbs.

"And with every circuit-lighting high," Trident continued the conversation thread, "there would be an equally devastating low."

"Exactly." Laura leaned back in her plush armchair exposing just how pregnant she really was. "And if Ms Boyard is a regular user of this drug or something like it, who knows what her thought processes are and what her next move might be."

I took a deep breath. It was all becoming very convoluted. To me, at least, the next move was simple, remove Boyard, and plant some hints that Laura had another property up for sale in the Central Business District. We could turn this situation in to a win for everybody, except whose who had already lost their lives, of course.

It really felt like a bit of a shame to have to kill someone else. Boyard and I had gotten on very well during our meeting and this week had already been a bit of a bloodbath. But things were escalating very quickly. I feared the situation was about getting out of hand. And post the attempt on my life, my support for Boyard's safety and continued existence was waning rapidly.

After a brief discussion, it appeared that I was not alone in this thought. But even in a room full of ruthless killers, there was reluctance to take another life. Not just because of the moral implications, but a spree of killings like this would force the authorities to come down hard on the areas affected. It would be unlikely that anyone would be arrested, but we would all have to be on our best behaviour for a month or two until the heat died down, and that would mean loss of revenue.

I changed the subject. "Well, if we are done here talking about the murder of poor, innocent, drug dealers, I would really love to see what you have in the way of pistols."

Laura stood up and waddled to the door way, being invisibly shadowed and assisted by PA Steve. "Sure," she smiled her half-smile, "step into my office." She made a welcoming gesture with her arms.

One and a half hours and a Glock 17 later, we were back in the barn and I was back in my bed. The meds the clinic doc gave me were great, but mostly just to help me sleep, I wasn't in too much pain. I took a pill and washed it down with the remains of a bottle of water.

Laura had given me a great deal on the Glock and some accessories, and even let me take it with me there and then, maybe feeling a little guilty for her part of me losing my beloved Beretta. But the only thing that is constant is change, and we have to embrace the new. I drifted off to a deep sleep, replaying the excitement of the past week in my dreams.

Chapter 15: A Knife to a Gun Fight

Your uphill struggle consumes you,
But can't seem to grasp the fact,
That you are living the life of Reilly,
That the wind is at your back.

Dave Milliken

1 August 2022

It was just after 0200hrs and Trident started knocking furiously on my door. "Get up, Blades. We need to go." Whatever was happening, it was clearly urgent.

I struggled from my bed, dressing with some difficulty. The bruise that seemed to consume the left-hand side of my shoulder and torso had turned a nasty yellow. The pain, which I thought I was already over, was starting to seep through the medication. Even though it hadn't been too bad, I had a sneaking feeling it was going to get a whole lot worse.

"Come on! Come on! Let's go!" Trident encouraged, banging on my door again with renewed vigour.

I stumbled from my room, finally dressed. "You know, it is a good job that I wasn't shot not a week ago."

"They have attacked Luke." Trident said, pulling weapons and ammunition from our gun locker.

All humour disappeared. "What?" I said, "When?"

"About 20 minutes ago."

"Help me with this." I requested as I tried in vain to pull on some form fitting anti-ballistic armour. Trident looked at me in annoyance then, realising that I had been shot not that long ago, came to my rescue.

Twenty minutes later, Trident was in the driving seat, and we were on our way to Cool Hand Lukes shooting range.

On our approach, we could see evidence of the carnage. A plume of black smoke licked with red and yellow flickers of fire against a backdrop of the night sky. Somehow it appeared worse out here in the countryside, away from the light pollution of the big city. We parked up 200 metres away and made the rest of the journey on foot. I had my new Glock strapped to my side and I could almost feel the anticipation of the ADS slung across the front of my chest. The form fitting body armour was uncomfortable, but it was displacing most of its weight on to my hips, and it was holding the rest of me in place.

As we drew closer, Trident released a sigh of relief. The smoke and fire we had noticed on our approach was coming from a vehicle burning happy on the road in front of the range. It looked like it had been hit by some sort of anti-tank missile.

"Hello, there!" Luke called out from a position even my low light compensators hadn't picked out yet. "What took you so long? Was it Blades driving? He drives like an Amish pensioner, you know!"

With our guard still up, we walked past the destroyed vehicle. It looked like some sort of makeshift Armour Personnel Carrier. I turned my head away when I noticed what remains of the driver was still sitting in the driver seat clutching the steering wheel. I didn't need any more nightmare material just right now.

"There are 2 over on the left as well Blades. No. Your other left." Luke called out again, mockingly, still from his hiding position.

I looked to my left and could make out 2 lifeless figures partially hidden by the undergrowth, adored in off-the-shelf combat clothing. And just to the right of them was a very familiar looking inhaler. I picked it up in a gloved hand and placed it in my long coat pocket.

We still weren't keen to call out to Luke in response. We weren't sure how many attackers might be left. The last thing we wanted was to give our position away. Luke was hidden, really well hidden too, so we were happy to allow him to give the instructions.

"I think I got all of them."

Yeah, Luke, I thought, famous last words.

But, as the sun started to rise, it seemed he had gotten them all, or the attackers he didn't manage to kill had headed for the hills. Luke had emerged from his hiding place as we approached the front door of the range. He had built a small, single person, bunker complete with CCTV and a simple plumbing system and sunk it into the ground. As he climbed out of his hide, he had to toss out the spent launching system of the LAW first. So much for not keeping illicit firepower.

"Are these friends of yours, Luke?" Trident waved the barrel of his rifle around the area of engagement.

"Hardly. Hang on...", he stopped in his tracks and Trident and I both tensed. Then he looked at me, shining a torch onto my damaged long coat, "What on earth happened to you?"

"It's a long story." I replied, not sure if I wanted to go through it all again.

"Well, I can't wait to hear about it. Who wants some coffee?"

In the office and over coffee and yellow pack custard cream biscuits, we filled Luke in on the adventures of the past couple of weeks. Not normally one to want to hear of such events, now it had arrived at his own door, Luke was all ears.

Luke topped up the coffees and placed another packet of brandless biscuits onto the table. "Despite being late and missing all the action, I really do appreciate you guys responding."

"I think there might be a connect between what happened to us in the Breakfast Shack and your uninvited guests." I said, retrieving a napkin from the table and reaching into my pocket.

"Oh yeah?" Trident helped himself to another biscuit.

"Yeah. I found this in the forest close to one of your expired friends. I reckon, if we searched the bodies, we would find more, just like it. Do you recognise this, Luke?" I place the drug inhaler upon the table, careful to not make bare skin contact with it.

He looked at it for a moment, as if searching his memory banks for something of resemblance. "No, no I do not. What is it?"

"It's an inhaler, Luke. It's a new way for the youth of today to experience mood enhancing substances. And there is definitely no other reason why you would be targeted? You haven't particularly annoyed anyone lately, have you? I mean, more than usual?"

Luke smiled, still studying the inhaler in great detail. "No, no. I mean, I don't think so. I have some powerful friends but I am just a small fish, albeit, a heavily armed small fish. Something like this just don't make any sense. They would have been more effective showing up during office hours, posing as potential members, and then just shooting me in the head."

"That's how I would do it." Trident joked.

Chapter 16: The Truth Will Set You Free

Only six figures in your pay packet,
And accepting your friends' success is tough,
You cannot cope with life's abundance,
Because daddy didn't love you enough.

Dave Milliken
01 August 2022

"That would have been a novel idea." A new voice entered the room and none of us had noticed Burkie, in his usual 3-piece suit, appear at the office doorway. Behind him stood 2 guards dressed in commando style of the shelf combat gear, looking like they were spoiling for a fight.

"Burkie..." Trident started, the legs of his chair scrapping against the floor as he pushed himself back from the table.

Burkie raised his arms in front of him in a soothing gesture, as if spreading calm throughout the room. "Now calm down, gentlemen. There is no need for any further bloodshed. I just wanted to stop by to thank you. Thank you for helping us test our new performance enhancing drug." He stepped forward and lifted the inhaler from the table. "Still needs a bit of work, huh, boys?" He cast a look over his shoulder at his two foot soldiers, who ignored him. "I did tell them that." He added, as if he was letting us in on a big secret. "You will, of course, be paid for your trouble and I know it was a bit mean of me not to let you in on the joke. But, you see, we needed to see how it worked in the wild, and you gentlemen, well, you presented the opportunity for a live test. In truth, I am kind of happy it wasn't a success. I have grown to like you. You are entertaining."

I sat with my rage rooting me to the spot. "So, what about Laura? What about Big Idea? Was that you too?"

"Ah! No. That was a happy accident. But Laura and I have come to an agreement, so you won't have to worry there. As for Big Idea, it was my team who suggested the paramilitary alliance in the first place. The ignorance and tenacity of Ms Boyard was just the right amount of smoke screen. Do you really think Big Idea needs offices in the Belfast CBD before floating on the stock exchange?" He scoffed. "Of course not. But it also provided the perfect front to eliminate that total psychopath, Tucker. Jason is much more amenable. Isn't he, Blades?"

I exchanged looks with Trident. This was all too much.

"So, I have done my drugs tests,", Burkie continued like he was marking off items on a checklist, "removed a dangerous man from a local militia, provided care and support for a soon to be working single mother, and..." He snapped his fingers as if he had forgotten something, "Oh, yes! Evicted the tenants from my barn." He smiled again, "Happy house hunting fellas, I really do wish you the best of luck".

And with that, he was gone.

The truth will set you free, but first it will piss you off.

Chapter 16: The Truth Will Set You Free

Unregulated

About the Author

Dave Milliken is a freelance consultant in the world of healthcare and informatics, working closely with both government and private organisations. He is passionate about making sure that people  using social and healthcare services are not left out of the decision-making process, at all levels and in organisations of all sizes.

Dave is the co-founder of the Belfast Co-production Learning and Develop team, and works closely with the Belfast Trust training team to ensure that people who use services are at the core of course creation, development, and delivery.

In his spare time, he chairs and co-chairs several groups whose main aim is giving an effective and meaningful voice to those with additional healthcare or social care needs and has developed support systems, both in architecture and software, for healthcare and social services.

You can learn more about Dave's work at:

www.BrainForHire.co.uk
Twitter: davemilliken0

Printed in Great Britain
by Amazon